"Powerful! *94 Maidens* is destined to teach you something you didn't already know about this horrific period in history. A compelling and significant novel of courage, faith, hope and love."

—Tamar Adini, retired Chair of the Hebrew, Jewish Studies, and Foreign Language Departments at Akiba Hebrew Academy in Pennsylvania, consultant for the Central Agency for Jewish Education, and mentor in the worldwide Neta-Avichai project.

"A lovingly and deftly crafted book that tells a poignant, shattering story. It is a beautiful homage and gift to a family who will never be forgotten."

—Anne Dubuisson Anderson, writing and publishing consultant

"Rhonda Fink-Whitman takes us on a search to find the truth about a family's past. In doing so, we discover some truths about ourselves. *94 Maidens* is a riveting journey."

—Rick Domeier, television personality and author of *Can I Get a Do Over?*

Tania Fink

# 94 Maidens

*Educate yourself*
*Teach others*

A Novel Inspired by True Events

by Rhonda Fink-Whitman

*With Love,*

*Rhonda Fink-Whitman*

First published by Dog Ear Publishing
4010 W. 86th Street, Ste H
Indianapolis, IN 46268
www.dogearpublishing.net

ISBN: 978-1-4575-1277-3

This book is printed on acid-free paper.

This story is based on actual events. In certain cases, incidents, characters, and timelines have been changed for dramatic purposes. Names of
certain people, businesses, and organizations have been changed to protect their privacy. Certain characters and events may be entirely ficti-
tious.

Referenced locations and landmarks in this novel are real. The ITS exists.

Printed in the United States of America

On the cover:
*There is no love in the world like a mother's love.*

—The inscription (translated from Hebrew) on the silver bracelet on the author's wrist, a treasured gift from her daughter, purchased while traveling in the land of Israel.

—The Joel Family Photo

*For Meine Mutti*

# ACKNOWLEDGMENTS

With enduring gratitude and everlasting love to:

- ~ my partner in everything, the love of my life, the man who has a hot cup of tea waiting for me every morning and has read my book almost as many times as I have, my safe place to land at the end of the day, my devoted husband, Mike, in whose arms I find my refuge, after all.

- ~ my first reader and most insightful editor, the kid who got dragged along but hopefully is all the better for it, my son, Josh.

- ~ the girl I could always count on for an unwaivering opinion, who teaches me something new each and every day, whether I'm ready or not, my daughter, Shayna.

- ~ my inspiration, the woman who taught me the greatest love of all which has brought me many blessings, my resilient, wonderful mother, with undying love and admiration for all that you've overcome and the legacy that you leave.

~ and to all of my friends and family who have cheered me on, continuously pumped me up, and been my sounding board throughout this entire writing process – you know who you are.

In loving memory of:

~ my grandparents, the ones I knew and the one I never got the chance to know, my cousins, great aunts, those who suffered at the hands of the Nazis and those who defied them and finally, to my dad who instilled in me the foundation of my faith and taught me that although "It's tough to be a Jew in America," it's a lot tougher elsewhere.

All of you are always with me.

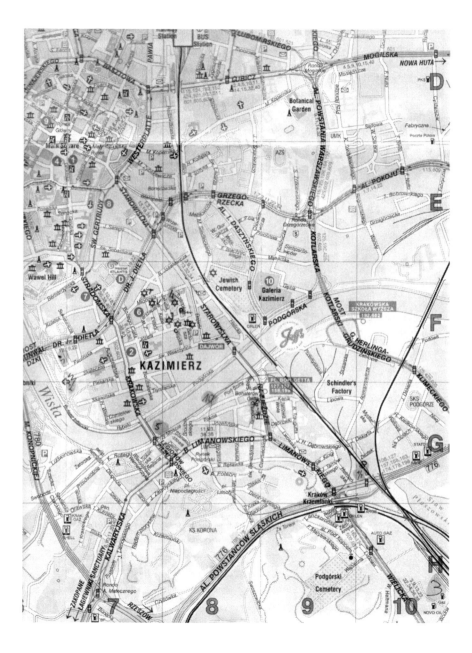

*The one who does not remember history is bound to live through it again.*

—George Santayana
The Life of Reason, Volume 1, 1905

# Prologue

NAZI-OCCUPIED POLAND
AUGUST 11, 1942

*T*he room was silent.

Purples, pinks, and azure blues from the late summer sunset streaked in through the somewhat smudged ceiling-to-floor dining room windows framed in rich golden paisley pique fabrics.

A large group of schoolgirls dressed in oddly matching white cotton nightgowns and ranging in age from 14 to 22 were both seated and standing around a long, deep cherry wood table draped in hand-laced linens. Each girl held a sparkling champagne flute crafted from precision-cut Bohemian crystal. The glasses were half-filled with water.

Fine, expensive European antique fixtures surrounded them, but the furniture was bare. Where sterling silver objects and heirloom artifacts once most certainly occupied a proud place on the fancy buffet and in the tall glass china cabinet, surfaces were now empty. On the walls, broken nails protruded from vacant spots where magnificent works by the masters had once hung.

The girls' teacher, a plain, worn-looking woman in her mid 40s, her mousy brown hair up in a neat, soft bun, sat focused at the head of the table. All eyes were on her. Concentrating hard to keep her slender, youthful-looking hands from shaking, she gently broke a transparent capsule over a glass of water and swirled it. As the powder dissolved, she spoke with a steady, quiet compassion. "That's all you need."

One by one, the young women followed her lead, carefully breaking capsules into their water, swirling the contents and intently watching the nearly imperceptible fusion of solids and liquid.

The oldest girl, exceptionally pretty with shoulder-length chestnut hair, proceeded around the room holding a crisp, white paper bag, collecting the remnants. A cascade of petite fingers unapologetically discarded each empty shell into the bag as it passed gracefully by. One missed, however, and landed somewhere on the beautiful table. No one noticed.

"Is everyone ready?" the teacher asked resolutely.

Nearly in synch, the girls nodded a solemn confirmation.

Steadying her glass, the teacher lovingly slipped a free arm inside the arm of the girl next to her. The girl next to her instinctively repeated the gesture with the girl next to *her* and so on until everyone was linked around the room.

The youngest girl, fair-haired and angelic, seated at the very far end of the table, could contain herself no longer. Ever so softly, she began to sob.

# Chapter 1

*T*ired hands shook vigorously as arthritically deformed fingers struggled to break a gelatin-coated capsule over a glass of water, releasing a white powder into the clear elixir.

This had become routine for my 70-year-old mother, whom my children call Bubbie. We had just finished an early dinner in one of those typical suburban chain family restaurants. Bubbie was looking good for her age, I thought. Her short, wavy red hair with blond highlights capped off her small, slightly padded body. She maintained her long, squared-off acrylic nails in a frosted shade of mauve. She always said that colorful, attractive nails would distract people from noticing her diseased, misshapen fingers, a trick she had learned from *her* aging mother. That was the thing about Bubbie— she usually looked better than she felt.

On any given day, at any given moment, Bubbie could be flexible or stubborn. In fact, the older she got, the more she resembled her mother, both physically and temperamentally. Watching the transformation unfold was indeed an eye-opening experience.

At the table, next to Bubbie, sat my two children. My son, Josh, 17, was tall, slim, and too smart for his own good. The dark peach fuzz on his chin and above his upper lip underscored his soulful brown eyes. Lazy but thoughtful, Josh was the affectionate one.

Next to Josh sat his 14-year-old sister, Shayna, a "don't touch me" princess, beautiful with her long, straight, luminous hair. Today it happened to be buttercup blond. Shayna used her babysitting money to spoil herself and was, as per usual, dressed from head to toe in overpriced name-brand attire from the mall. Despite my best efforts to the contrary, Josh and Shayna both possessed an air of teenage entitlement. I could only hope they'd outgrow it. Soon.

On my side of the table was my uber-supportive husband, Mike, a big guy, tough, steadfast, in his late 40s. We'd been married 23 years. Mike was everything I wasn't. He was the yang to my yin. An IT guy, he was the left side of the brain to my right. If one of us had a problem, the other had the solution. He was the provider, the rock, and not an anniversary went by that I didn't get flowers *and* a poem. Yeah, I was a lucky girl.

Then there was me. The everywoman. I liked to describe myself as approachable: real good at making eye contact, friendly, sincere, and pleasant-looking enough that total strangers felt comfortable engaging me in conversation—in the supermarket, in an airport, just about anywhere.

I had learned over the years how to make the most of what I'd been given. Ever mindful of my clock ticking dangerously close to 50, I watched what I ate, kept "the girls" hoisted, the waist cinched, and took my wardrobe cues from my daughter, dressing in a tastefully modified adult version of what she and her friends thought was currently hot. It was definitely working for me, because everyone said I'd never looked better. And I had the soft-focused Facebook pictures to prove it.

All things considered, life was pretty damn good.

Bubbie contorted her shoulders as she discarded the empty capsule onto a used napkin on the table. A chunky gold charm bracelet dangled from her wrist. It had lots of baubles. They caught the light.

Realizing I hadn't said the traditional Hebrew blessing over the wine, I lifted my glass, which still had a drop of Riesling left in it, and abbreviated the recitation. "Oops, almost forgot," I apologized. *"Boray p'ree hagafen,* Creator of the fruit of the vine."

My family responded with the obligatory what-she-said, "Amen."

Mike picked up the empty capsule and examined it curiously. "What's this for?" he asked.

Bubbie replied, "Pain."

A young, timid waitress approached the table with a credit card and placed the slip down for a signature. Bubbie gently touched the waitress's arm. "Hon, could you please bring me a box?"

We glanced at Bubbie's plate. Only about a fork-full of veggie lasagna remained.

Shayna rolled her eyes. Josh chuckled.

Like a mother tiger, I snarled my disapproval at my cubs as I reached for and signed the check. "Don't start," I admonished.

But Mike felt the need to chime in. "C'mon, there's nothing left!"

The waitress quietly shrank away.

Fuming, I slammed the check down on the table.

I've always been inherently protective of my mother. You only get one, and this one was wincing. "Sorry, Mom," I said, offering her a sandbag in preparation for the storm. She feigned a smile.

Josh whispered to his sister, "Here we go."

It was then that I lost it. My subsequent tirade was familiar. "You know she can't throw out food, and you know why," I shouted, launching into a fire-breathing repertoire.

"Actually, we don't. She never talks about it," Shayna interrupted.

"She can't," I insisted.

"Can't or won't?" Josh wanted to know.

Bubbie jumped in apologetically. "Both," she said before excusing herself to the ladies' room.

Every bone in my mother's weary body creaked as she peeled herself out of the booth. I waited for her to be out of earshot before I continued my disciplinary rant.

"Don't *ever* judge her."

"That was soooooo long ago," Josh whined.

"Seriously, Mom," Shayna had the chutzpah to add. "Why should we care?"

"What *does* it have to do with us?" their unenlightened father had the gall to contribute.

I could have spit blood. "Are you kidding me?! None of you has any idea what she's been through."

Mike threw up his hands. "Really, Rhonda? Well, neither do you."

Bubbie returned to the table, saw that we were still arguing, and shivered. She was starting to show her age, I realized.

"You know what...you're right," I said, completely vexed. "It's about time I found out."

I noticed our waitress taking an order at another table. "Get her the damn box!" I shouted in her direction. The waitress pouted, so I tempered my frustration with, "Please."

My family seemed somewhat befuddled.

"So, now you're on a mission?" Shayna wondered out loud.

"What are you lookin' for?" Josh asked.

Bubbie swirled her glass. "The truth," she answered for me, then threw back the rest of her drink.

Impatiently, I gathered my belongings. "Let's go. I have to be at work in two hours!"

The waitress returned with the box and anxiously placed it on the table.

Mike grew a bit worried. "You've been toying with the idea for years, but we can't let you go alone."

"Wait, what?" Josh asked.

"Don't look at me," Shayna said emphatically. "I'm goin' to overnight camp this summer."

Mike and I stared at Bubbie, who was busy packing up her leftovers. "Oh, no. I could never..." she protested.

We turned toward Josh. His head fell toward the table. "Crap, I got nothin.'"

I bolted up out of my seat and pointed to my watch. If steam had actually been coming from my ears, it would have certainly fogged up the nearest window.

"Ticktock!" I demanded, finally succeeding in getting them to hightail it out of their chairs.

I caught my impatient reflection in the glass of the door as we passed through it on our way out of the restaurant. At this particular moment, I knew a lot of things. I knew that what I had to tackle was long overdue and time was not on my side. Evidence was turning to dust, history was being rewritten, and Mom and others like her weren't getting any younger. But what I did *not* know and couldn't possibly fathom was how the journey on which I was about to embark would reshape who I thought I was and so profoundly change my life forever.

But first, I *really* had to get to work.

# Chapter 2

*T*he Shop From Home Network studio was brightly lit and bustling with activity. Behind the scenes of the nationally televised channel, back-stage crew members scurried to and fro with headsets and clipboards and floor people diligently shuffled monitors with long thick cables from set to set. Cameras moved robotically as they were remotely positioned by unseen directors in a state-of-the-art second-floor booth. In the stylishly re-created living room, a 40ish, bouncy program host was selling colorful pre-curled ribbons. Nearby, in the efficient-looking "craft room," standing behind a long rolling table, I was putting the finishing touches on my setup. I placed a pre-made scrapbook page on a small clear Gibson stand, then adjusted my snug-fitting sweater over my knee-length pencil skirt and checked the non-skid heels on my favorite high-heeled cocoa leather boots.

Securing the earpiece comfortably in my left ear, I heard the director. "Coming to you next, Rhonda. Thirty seconds."

I took a deep breath and put on my best camera-ready smile.

Just in time, the female host from the next set, Jamie, approached the table and gave me a quick hug. She was exotically pretty, and it wasn't hard to see how she had landed a job in television. "Hey babe, good to work with you again," she said in a bubbly sort of way. "Here we go."

Jamie looked directly into Camera 3. "Okay, crafters, my old friend and longtime Shop From Home guest Rhonda Fink-Whitman is here with a fantastic paper trimmer that lights up!"

I held the trimmer up to the handheld camera and demonstrated by flipping the light on and off repeatedly.

"That's right, Jamie," I said, launching into my soft, neighborly, over-the-backyard-fence spiel that had made me a successful electronic retailer for the past ten years. "The light is the key...completely takes the guesswork out of trimming so you can make a precision cut every time," I declared, taking both ownership and pride in the product. It was more of a friendly explanation than a hard sell. My early years as a radio personality, gracing the Philadelphia airwaves with everything from traffic and news reports to stints as a weekend jock and even as a morning show co-host, had laid the foundation for this coveted gig. My friends would joke that I could sell ice cubes to Eskimos in the winter. I would retort, "Only if I really liked the ice cubes." My pitch was always passionate but sincere.

"Let me show you how it works..." I went on to slice and dice a variety of photos, pieces of card stock, and blocks of text and after a few minutes returned to the pre-made scrapbook page and removed it from the Gibson stand. "If we could get a closer look at this page I've made, you'll see all of the decorative edges..." I began to run my meticulously manicured nails in my favorite shade-Cajun Spice—over each and every scallop and perforation.

Jamie cut me off before the camera had a chance to zoom in on the page or the ten-dollar manicure.

"The light-up paper trimmer has just sold out!" she announced. "Rhonda, thank you so much for being here at our big scrapbooking event today."

I shook Jamie's hand and smiled broadly. "Don't forget it comes with eleven interchangeable safety blades," I responded in my affable, on-air manner.

Jamie furrowed her brow and moved to her next sell in the "bedroom."

"They're all gone, Rhonda," said the voice in my ear. "Give it a rest."

Looking up at the director's booth, I shrugged. "I'm pre-selling the next order," I replied with a wink at the man behind the curtain.

I pulled the earpiece from my ear.

"Whoo hoo!"

I didn't need to look up to know who was approaching my table. I recognized the voice right away.

Valerie was another Shop From Home on-air guest, the liaison between the vendors, the network, and me and was the person directly responsible for scheduling my airings. An effervescent, attractive, 50-year-old blonde with a touch of ADD, she dove right in to help me break down my set and pack up my supplies.

"Way to sell out, RFW!" she exclaimed. "Great job, as always. You sold me!"

"Thanks, but maybe you're an easy sell."

"Maybe *you're* a born closer."

I laughed.

"Hey, wanna stop for a pomegranate martini on the way home?" she continued excitedly.

"Sorry. Can't," I regretfully responded as I flicked all of the lights off on the sample trimmers. "Got an early class tomorrow."

"Still teaching religious school?"

"Yep."

We packed the remaining trimmers and samples into a large rolling cart with a long sturdy handle.

Valerie seemed both supportive and interested. "Cool! What's on the lesson plan?" she asked enthusiastically.

I shot her a somber look. "The Holocaust."

"Ouch. What a job." Val winced.

I felt the need to explain as we crammed the last of my supplies tightly into the cart. "Rabbi says we're 'making Jews.' For me, that's not a job, it's a responsibility."

At that moment, I realized I was still holding the scrapbook page that I had removed from the Gibson stand a few minutes earlier. I stared at it intently.

On it was a photocopy of an old sepia family portrait. In the picture stood a dapper, self-confident-looking gentleman, a dark-haired woman with a worried smile, and a doe-eyed, porcelain-skinned, beautiful little girl. In a bold, legible font, the title on the page read "Hitler's Berlin."

My eyes welled up.

# Chapter 3

*A*bout a year earlier, I had learned of a facility in Germany called the International Tracing Service. This was the secret agency where all of the Nazi documents had been collected, categorized, filed, stored, and sealed since the close of WWII. The ITS, as it was often called, was sort of a mythical place. Everyone knew of its existence, but no one ever dared to seek it out. It was buried somewhere deep in the heart of Deutschland, shrouded in mystery, cloaked in rumor, and historically unattainable by mere mortals like me.

Originally and officially run by the Allies post-WWII, the ITS was now kept under lock and key by its German gatekeepers, who had amassed over the past sixty-some years the largest, most complete Nazi archive the world had *never* seen.

Armed with only bits and pieces of information reluctantly relayed to me after sufficient badgering of certain relatives, I emailed the ITS, asking if they could please help fill in some of the blanks, details of what had happened to my family members during the Holocaust.

After about six months, I received a response telling me they could not release any information without a signature. So I penned a new request, signed it, and faxed it back.

Another six months passed without a reply, and finally, I decided it was time to just go there—or at least *try* to go there. I had always known that I had come out of the ashes of the Holocaust, and for some reason, I felt it was my *duty* to see with my own eyes what had been done to my family and how it had been done. I felt there was no other way to comprehend the madness. I had read about it, seen documentaries, watched everything that even hinted of Hitler on the History Channel, and taught Holocaust studies to my fifth and sixth-grade students at my synagogue's religious school, but still I had this unrequited drive to go to the concentration camps; stand on the train tracks; see, hear, feel everything. Bear witness. I owed it to my family, to the six million. I owed it to myself.

Now, just a couple of days before my long-awaited trek to Europe, I decided that I needed some extra guidance, or maybe just an authoritative nod that I was doing the right thing and that it would be okay.

I circled around my cozy bedroom, haphazardly packing. The room remained mostly in order, save for a small clump of dirty laundry piled in the corner next to the large picture window that overlooked a secluded wooded backyard. An open, well-traveled, empty black suitcase was sprawled out on the neatly made bed. I erratically went through drawers, pulling out panties and bras and tossing them into the suitcase. My cell phone was sandwiched snugly between my right ear and shoulder.

The voice I heard on the other end of the line was pleasant at first. "United States Holocaust Memorial Museum, Archives Department. How may I help you?"

I got right to the point. "I have a question about the International Tracing Service in Germany," I began. "You know, the place where they keep all of the Nazi records..."

The reply was quick. "I am very familiar."

I threw a few more random articles of clothing into the luggage: a couple of button-down blouses, an all-purpose black gauze skirt, a pair of jeans.

"About a year ago, I sent them an email requesting information about my family members and still have not received a response."

"No surprise there."

The reaction caught me off guard. I stopped packing. "What do you mean?"

"They are backlogged with 400,000 requests for information," the archivist explained.

"You're telling me I'm number 400,001?"

I didn't know whether to laugh or cry.

"The Germans have kept those records sealed—"

I interrupted. "Yeah, I know, but—"

The archivist continued, "During the last seven years, this museum and the Yad Vashem memorial in Jerusalem have been putting pressure on them to make the documents public. They may finally begin releasing a portion of the records next fall."

"What the hell is taking so long?" I asked impatiently. I noticed that I was now talking with my hands.

"Everything has to be translated and digitized...it'll be a while before you can learn anything about your family."

"Listen..." I said as I picked up three passports from the dresser. "I'm going to Germany. What do you think would happen if I just knocked on the door and asked them to show me what they have?" Seemed simple enough to me.

I examined the passports closely—mine, Mike's, and Josh's. I triple-checked the expiration dates and exhaled.

"No one gets in," the archivist stated flatly and without hesitation. "Not researchers, not writers, not reporters. Survivors don't get past the front lobby."

"But—" I challenged.

"Don't," the archivist warned. "They'll slam the door in your face."

"We'll see about that," I said as I hung up the phone.

I tossed the passports into an accessible front pocket and forced the suitcase shut. After sitting on top of it and successfully coaxing the reluctant zipper from one end to the other, I secured a heavy-duty TSA lock.

I grinned. This wasn't over.

Unable to sleep at 1:30 a.m. and unsatisfied with the orders I had received from the representative at the

United States Holocaust Memorial Museum, I crawled out of bed, stepped into my home office, and got online to see what I could do to prove her wrong. From a transcript of a recent television segment on the ITS, I learned the name of the chief archivist in charge of maintaining the sealed Nazi documents. After a little further research, I had a proper email address for this man. I fired off a quick note and crawled back into bed.

By the time I awoke, around 8:00 a.m., I had an answer from Germany.

"Dear Mrs. Fink-Whitman," the email read in perfect English. "There are documents on hand here…of course you can examine them on the occasion of your visit…I hope that this meets with your wishes and remain with friendly greetings…"

My hands shook as I picked up the phone and dialed Mike's cell. Already on his way to work, he was stuck in rush-hour traffic on the Pennsylvania Turnpike when he answered, via Bluetooth, "What's up?"

"Honey," I squealed, unable to contain my excitement, "We're in!"

# Chapter 4

*M*etal rubbing together squeaked faintly as giant black steel doors closed and locked behind me, Mike, Josh, and our tall, aloof German guide, Rolf.

Balding, with a white beard and mustache trimmed neatly close to his face and a small diamond stud in his left ear, at the ripe age of 66, Rolf towered, ominous and expressionless, above everyone else.

For a moment, the group of us stood encased in a foreboding silence. Hovering in a blank canvas of a foyer, we could see nothing, no one. A flag, pure white with a large red cross off center, protruding over our heads from the doorpost was our only companion. We looked around at the colorless walls and at each other, feeling vulnerable and a bit lost. "We're not in Kansas anymore," I quietly joked in a desperate attempt to self-comfort. I tried to disguise it as lightening the mood for the benefit of my husband and my son, but I don't think anyone was buying it.

Finally, the sound of heels clicking along the pristine marble floor interrupted the silence like a rapid flurry of pebbles against a glass window. A tailored-looking woman in her late 40s with short-cropped blond hair and a somber mouth approached. "We've been expecting you. Welcome to the International Tracing Service. I'm Frau Weisz. This way, *bitte*, please."

Frau Weisz led us past a security desk through a spacious but sparse two-story lobby. In the lobby were a few displays. Personal belongings beckoned to us from behind glass: documents, photos, wedding bands, a man's pocket watch, a woman's makeup compact, a gold necklace strung with twinkling emerald-green gems. On the wall, behind the mementoes, hung a very large map. "Deutschland Unter der Hitler-Diktatur 1933–1945," it read. On it, every concentration camp in Europe under the Hitler dictatorship was conspicuously marked with a large blue Star of David. Anxiously, I stayed close by Frau Weisz's side. Josh and Mike lagged somewhat behind. Rolf brought up the rear.

Josh put his arm around his father and leaned in to whisper, "How the hell did Mom get us inside this place?"

Mike whispered back, "She asked nicely."

"*Nicely?* That's it?"

"She always says she gets more bees with honey than with vinegar. Your mom happens to be very sweet."

Somewhat annoyed at their turtle-slow pace, I turned and hustled them. "Keep up! Let's go!" I snapped.

"*My* mom?" Josh cracked.

Rolf snickered.

Frau Weisz stopped us at the entrance to a vast, well-lit room. The walls were lined back to back with alcoves. Each alcove contained floor-to-ceiling vaults. I could see that the vaults were labeled alphabetically by concentration camp and were on rolling tracks so that with the unlocking and turning of a three-pronged steel wheel, they could be slid apart to allow access to their secrets. Frau Weisz explained that inside each vault were shelves packed air-tight with binder after binder. Every binder was catalogued and organized by year. Each one was stuffed with either typed or handwritten original papers documenting everything the Nazis had chosen to record. Even the center of the room was covered with large and small filing cabinets. Every single drawer was meticulously tagged. There wasn't much space for a person to maneuver. This room was designed for papers. I later learned that if you laid out the documents contained within and walked from beginning to end, you would travel 16 miles.

Our jaws hit the floor.

"Holy crap," Josh said under his breath.

"We *are* in!" exclaimed Mike.

I looked around in awe, almost unable to speak. "So this is where all of the Nazi secrets have been hiding for over 60 years," I finally uttered.

Even Rolf felt compelled to remark. "*Scheisse*," he said under his breath.

A new voice from behind us spoke English fluently, with less of a distinct German accent than we had become accustomed to hearing since boarding our Lufthansa flight to Frankfurt.

"Information on 17 million people...most of them victims of Nazi atrocities, but also lots of documents on the perpetrators themselves," the man attested.

We turned to see a slightly disheveled fellow in his late thirties. He was a bit on the pudgy side, with a salt-and-pepper beard and mustache, and was wearing a plaid navy shirt with a red, white, and blue-striped tie. The man's face was extremely warm and friendly. I wondered if the tie choice had anything to do with our visit.

Instinctively, I put out my hand. "You must be Otto."

As he shook my hand, he confirmed, "Chief archivist of the International Tracing Service, Otto Lehrer. Nice to meet you."

I eagerly made the introductions. "Rhonda Fink-Whitman. My husband, Mike, our son, Josh, and this is our guide, Rolf." I sighed as I gushed my overwhelming feelings of appreciation. "Thank you for letting us in."

Otto looked surprised. "Of course! As soon as I received your email, I looked up your family members, found their documents, and got them ready for your visit today." He beckoned. "Follow me."

Otto led us down a narrow aisle.

"Did you say you have information on Jews *and* Nazis?" Rolf asked.

Otto looked at Rolf and smiled uneasily. "Brace yourself," he instructed in German.

Otto stopped in front of a small filing cabinet. He opened the top drawer and pulled out a random folder. "Let me show you something."

He flipped through a ledger and revealed a page of it to his eager visitors. "You see this list? One of the concentration camps. Three hundred Jews randomly executed, one every two minutes until the job was done. April 20, 1943."

I didn't need to do the math. I knew exactly what that date meant. "Hitler's birthday," I noted.

"A gift for der Fuehrer," Otto confirmed.

Rolf looked shocked. "It's a shame so many Jews died in those camps."

We all stared at Rolf in utter disbelief. Had he really just made the understatement of the century? In this, of all places?

"Murdered," Otto sternly corrected.

"Well, not all of them were murdered," Rolf objected. "Some of them just died, right?"

Thank God Otto had the floor.

He grimaced. "If they weren't gassed or shot, they died of disease or starvation. The Nazis put them in those situations."

Despite their discrepancy in size, Otto managed to get right in Rolf's face. "Make no mistake about it, my friend. They were murdered. Every single one of them."

Rolf's head dropped. He mumbled something in his native tongue and left the room.

I looked at Otto. "What did he say?"

"He said they didn't teach that in school."

Otto escorted me, Mike, and Josh to a small, round wooden table with a couple of hard, sturdy chairs, the kind you'd find in an old classroom, I thought. As we took our seats around the table, Otto dropped a heavy folder in front of us.

"This is everything we have."

I reached into my backpack and pulled out the original copy of the old family photo from the Shop From Home scrapbook page and placed it gingerly on the table. "This is everything *we* have."

Otto smiled. I hesitated, waiting for his permission.

"Whenever you're ready," he greenlighted.

I stared at the manila folder for about a minute. It was thick. Certainly, lots of information was inside. I was filled with excitement and anticipation. Could the long-awaited answers *really* be in here, finally, right in front of me, at my fingertips? Were the horrors that had remained so unspeakable over the past 60 years amongst my surviving family members now actually within my grasp? My hands began to shake uncontrollably as I slowly, carefully peeled open the forbidden folder.

Glancing at the first page, I quickly grew flustered. My eyes glazed over, and I must have looked as if I were about to burst into tears, because my always-sensitive son seemed concerned. "Mom, what is it?"

"It's our "itinerary" for the next thirteen days," I said metaphorically.

I sat idle for a minute in a slight state of confusion. "I, I don't know," I finally stammered. "It's all in German." My eyes were drawn to the bottom of the page. "Wait!" I gasped. "I recognize the writing. Oh my God, the handwriting! I haven't seen that signature in years. It's..." I started to break down. "Regina's."

Otto gently took the folder from me. "I will translate," he soothingly assured.

I shook my head. The room was spinning. On the table in front of me, a pen and a notepad suddenly materialized. Mike zipped up my bag.

"Where do we start?" I wheezed, overcome with emotion and *fear,* real, undeniable fear. I hadn't anticipated that.

An unexpected voice returned. "At the beginning."

Surprised, we all looked up to find Rolf standing in the doorway of the cluttered room. Off the very tip of his index finger, dangling precariously, were the keys to his car.

# Chapter 5

KAZIMIERZ

*I*t was raining rather steadily in Berlin. Mike, Josh, and I practically tripped over each other struggling to share Rolf's only standard-size black umbrella as we followed him in line like baby ducks behind their mother. We scampered close behind in size order, which, by default, made me the caboose. On my toes, concentrating on stepping over rather large puddles, I could feel the wetness slide off the edge of the umbrella and trickle steadily down the back of my bare neck, soaking half of my beige cardigan sweater and everything underneath it. It mattered not.

I peeked at some notes I had made back at the ITS. "When Rolf said we were starting at the beginning, he wasn't kidding!" I called to Mike and Josh, speedily tucking the important papers back inside my pocket to keep them dry.

A few feet ahead, paying no mind to the foul weather beating down on his balding head and square shoulders, Rolf walked us into the center of an immense plaza located inside the courtyard of Humboldt University.

"This used to be called the Opernplatz," he explained.

He directed our attention to a thick Plexiglas window bolted directly into the cobblestone ground.

"This is an Israeli artist's rendering of what took place here," he continued.

We were quite surprised to hear the word "Israeli" while in Germany and had felt somewhat vindicated earlier in the day when we'd passed by streets named after Israeli dignitaries like Ben Gurion Strasse and Yitzchak Rabin Strasse.

Carefully, we knelt down on the wet surface, wiped some of the accumulated water off the window, and peered through to see endless wooden bookshelves. Every inch of them was bare.

I gazed sadly past the soaked veneer. The rain was driving down hard now, pelting the memorial.

"She used to love to read..." I remembered out loud.

# Chapter 6

MAY 10, 1933

*T*he night sky over Humboldt University was thick with smoke. Between the fumes and the rhetoric, German Jews found it nearly impossible to breathe.

Brownshirts, as they were called— high-ranking Nazi Stormtroopers in dusty brown uniforms, professors, and students alike were burning books in the Opernplatz outside Humboldt University.

Volume after volume written by Jewish authors and anyone else considered un-German was thrown into the mountainous piles being set ablaze in the center of the vast plaza. Publications by Freud and Hemingway, even the writings of Helen Keller went up in flames.

Bands played, songs were sung, people marched in torchlight parades, and fiery speeches were delivered.

A young couple—Manfred, tall, thin, and handsome at 23, and Regina, raven-haired and petite, 25— watched in horror from a somewhat safe distance.

She was clutching a book written by Heinrich Heine. On the back cover a quote was clearly visible. It read, "WHERE THEY BURN BOOKS, SO TOO WILL THEY IN THE END BURN HUMAN BEINGS. —HEINRICH HEINE, 1821"

Suddenly, a sneering young man racing by Regina grabbed her book and tossed it into the bonfire with joyous abandon. Regina clung to Manfred, with *both* hands.

# Chapter 7

BERLIN, 1938

*M*oonlight strained in through a dusty street-level window to shed some after-hours light on a small but well-equipped basement gym and fight club. The place was quiet, except for the repetitive sound of a punching bag taking a series of slow, deliberate blows. Heavy chains linked the bag to the ceiling.

A left fist hit the bag. Then a right. The momentum was lackluster. A few more punches landed, then a sigh rebounded off the stone walls of the empty facility.

Manfred, now 28, stood in a white undershirt, which showed off his tight abs, muscular shoulders, and strong arms. It was evident that, though a bit on the lean side, he was still an athlete who trained hard.

He took a step backward, fixated for a moment by the evening's early moonlight.

Within the past month, he had experienced several disturbing encounters. He recalled seeing a gaggle of well-dressed families with multiple bags, packed to the gills and bursting at the seams, converged on the Berlin city train station. It was a bit chaotic as patriarchs emptied their pockets of gold coins and other currency to pay for safe passage for their broods out of Germany. One by one, they lined up to show their ID cards to the German authorities. Each card was stamped with a big red J, identifying its holder as a Jew.

While walking through the business district, he had seen *Sturmabteilungen,* SA, thugs escort a third-generation Jewish store owner out of his own *schmatta* (fabric) shop. The humble man turned to see a new sign being unveiled over his old one, changing the name of his longtime family establishment from Schwartz's to Schmidt's.

Over in the center of the town, Manfred had watched as Nazis prevented a couple of men in suits with briefcases from entering the old courthouse. When the men questioned the action, the Nazis gleefully pointed out a sign posted on the large carved oak doors that read, "NO ENTRANCE FOR JEWISH LAWYERS!"

Manfred's old school chum, Dr. Werner Huber, an OB/GYN with a pleasant, kind, bespectacled face— just the sort of doctor anyone would choose to deliver their children—had told Manfred how he'd stood in silhouette in front of his sun-soaked office window to speak to a burly farmer from a nearby town, his pregnant wife, and their handful of young, well-behaved children.

"But, Dr. Huber," the man pleaded in a gruff, low voice to match his rough-looking exterior, "you've been our trusted physician for years...you delivered all of our *kinder*....why is it suddenly illegal for you to continue our treatment?"

The doctor slowly moved away from the window, revealing a large red Star of David that had been crudely painted on the outside pane of glass. The family looked surprised. As the doctor had come into focus from the shadows, he unequivocally replied, "I am a Jew."

Scanning the gym, Manfred noticed the thin layer of dirt that covered the floor. He walked deliberately to the corner of the room, bent down, and, with his index finger, scooped up some dust. Returning to the punching bag, he began to draw a fist-sized swastika dead center on the bag. He blew the remaining dust off his finger. A smirk crossed his handsome face.

Curling his fingers inward, he made a fist, pivoted, and punched, dead on the swastika, hard. Again. And again. Soon, he had a powerful rhythm going. He was hitting that bag as if Hitler himself were standing there, taking the punches. Manfred was focused and smiling now as he worked up a good sweat.

A teenaged boy appeared in the doorway of the gym. At 17, Erich was as eager, enthusiastic, and magnetic as a new puppy. Given his lanky but toned build, olive complexion, and mane of thick sable hair, even the older ladies couldn't resist pinching his blushed cheeks and tousling his silky locks whenever they had the good fortune of seeing him. Manfred had known the boy since Erich's birth. He was the only child of dear family friends who, unable to conceive for years, had their "miracle baby" late in life. Because Erich's parents were closer in age to that of grandparents and were among those Jews who had been able to secure early passage to America, promising to send for their son as soon as they settled, Manfred had taken the energetic youth under his wing.

The unthinkable idea of children being separated from their parents would soon become an unfortunate reality for many Jewish families desperate to stay together under Hitler's oppressive Third Reich. Erich was content to live in his parents' flat, finish his last year of formal education during the week, and work as Manfred's apprentice in his spare time. The two spent many hours together.

The boxer didn't notice the boy at first; he was too focused on the task at hand. Erich watched silently for a few moments as Manfred pummeled the bag. Manfred's determination both awed and amused him.

"Not by might nor by power, but by my spirit, says the Lord," Erich suddenly announced.

Manfred, startled, steadied the bag. He was just a bit out of breath. He smiled when he spotted Erich at the door. "The key to our survival. Perhaps not always as individuals, but together as a people. Survival comes in many forms, my boy," he responded.

"Yes, my all-knowing mentor," Erich replied sarcastically. "I will remember that."

Manfred smiled again, this time the smile mostly radiated from his kind, sparkling blue eyes. "What are you doing here?"

"Your wife said I would find you at the gym."

Manfred pounded the bag a few more times. His sweaty shoulders glistened in the scant light.

Erich glanced at his watch, then looked around curiously. There was no one else in the gym. "But, how did you...?"

"The owner, *Herr* Keller, is an old friend. He lets me practice after hours," Manfred explained, throwing another punch. He steadied the bag once more. "Why did she send you?"

Erich looked like the cat that had swallowed the canary. "Manfred," he said cheerfully, "it's time."

Manfred's smile broadened. He threw on his old, worn jacket.

"Hurry," Erich urged.

Manfred flew up the steps to meet Erich and patted his young protégé on the back. The two men raced out of the building and closed the door. A sign hanging on the inside window of the door swung back and forth. Dutifully, Manfred pulled a key out of his jacket pocket, locked the door, then quickly hid the key in the doorjamb. Manfred and Erich carefully looked left, then right, then at each other. It was all clear. Quietly laughing, they dashed off together into the dark, dangerous streets of Berlin.

The swinging sign on the door finally settled. Handwritten in German, it read, "JEWS AND DOGS UNWELCOME."

# Chapter 8

*T*he next stop, according to our ITS "blueprint," was Poland. I managed to save a sizeable chunk of change on airfare by booking us an internet flight through Denmark. Unfortunately, the layover was so extended that we probably could have walked from Germany and gotten there sooner.

At the Copenhagen airport, time was wasted, lunch cost way too many dik diks (Danish krones), and Mike and Josh were unhappy campers.

By the time we boarded the train to Krakow, they were over it.

A warm late-afternoon sun stuck around to welcome us when we finally reached the station. We struggled a bit to get our luggage onto the platform. A very tall, baby-faced blond man in his late twenties approached us almost immediately.

In a knee-jerk reaction, Mike protected his wallet. "What are you doing?" I asked.

"Rolf told me the pickpockets in Poland are the worst in all of Europe," he was quick to report.

"*Hallo!* Whitman family?" the young man asked before formally introducing himself. "I am Memel, your tour guide in Krakow." He had a pleasant smile and was friendly in a forced, polite sort of way.

We put down our bags to greet him.

Memel instinctively grabbed the handle on my suitcase and walked at a quick pace to his pearl-blue old-model Ford minivan, rolling my cumbersome black clamshell behind him. Mike, Josh, and I swiftly realized that we needed to put it into high gear to keep up with him. There was no time for jet lag.

"I have your itinerary here, and I see we are going to be very busy. We will drop your luggage at the hotel. Then, I leave it up to you. Where would you like to start?"

He loaded all of the pieces of luggage into the back of his van, tossing our suitcases in haphazardly but making sure he had just enough room to close the hatch.

I responded without hesitation, "The Beth Jacob School for Girls."

Memel slammed the trunk closed. His cheerful expression sobered. "What?" He looked over his paperwork. "I don't see that..."

"Do you know where it is?" I pressed him as I dug into my organized navy-blue travel satchel. Well, it was organized by *my* standards, anyway. "I have the address—"

Memel promptly interrupted me. "Number Ten Stanislava. Yes. I know. I am just, how you say, surprised."

"Why is that?" Josh asked.

"I've been a guide for ten years," Memel explained. "Tourists from every country ask me to take them to this place in Krakow and that. But *no one* has ever asked me about..."

*"Beth Jacob," Otto had read stoically from a page in the file. We didn't flinch; we barely breathed. We hung on his every word. Then he kindly explained, "It was a school for Jewish girls in Krakow."*

Mike made eye contact with me. I gave him "the look." After more than two decades of marriage, my intuitive hubby knew how to read my signals. Memel had been hired on a need-to-know basis, and until we felt we could trust him, our reasons for seeing this place or any other on our trip were personal and, at least for now, he didn't need to know.

Always my protector, Mike headed him off. "She's a teacher."

We waited to see if our guide had been placated.

Finally, Memel shrugged. He slid open the van's rear door and motioned us inside. "Okay," he conceded. "We go."

# Chapter 9

KAZIMIERZ

#10 STANISLAVA STREET,
BETH JACOB SCHOOL FOR GIRLS
LATE SEPTEMBER, 1938

*T*he dorm room was tiny and unassuming. A short stack of weathered suitcases sat piled neatly in the corner. Sarah admired her crisp, new framed teaching certificate and hung it on a bent nail protruding from the wall.

The teacher had a gentle face, an extra chin, and a slightly cherubic figure. Her brown hair was, as always, pulled back in a neat, soft bun.

She exuded a quiet confidence.

A white, short-haired cat with bright green eyes and a long tail cocked his head as he watched her from his comfortable spot on the bed.

"Long time coming, Ephraim," she admitted to the cat.

Effie softly meowed an acknowledgment.

Suddenly, Sarah heard a not-so-distant knock in the hallway.

She tiptoed across the room to the door. Her soft, beautiful hands, which did not reveal her forty-something years, reached for the knob.

In the hallway, Sarah could see a young student, fair-haired and angelic, with a thin beige blanket wrapped around her nightgown, knocking on the door directly across the hall.

The headmistress, Yetta Seweryna, emerged, opening her door halfway. She was rail thin and stern looking with her graying hair pulled back so tightly, Sarah could see the creases from her narrow eyes to her hairline. She was grimacing.

Undetected, Sarah watched silently as Yetta and the girl had a short, inaudible conversation. From her vantage point, she could tell that the headmistress was berating the girl.

Finally, Sarah watched helplessly as Yetta slapped the child across her face and slammed her door shut.

Sarah was horrified.

In front of the closed door, the dejected girl remained in the hallway for another unbearable moment. Sarah followed her gaze down toward the floor. There were drops of blood on the hard wood between her smooth, bare feet.

Sarah wrapped a lightweight, powder-blue robe around herself.

"I'll be back soon," she quietly informed the cat as she covertly slipped into the hallway.

The young girl had disappeared. Sarah followed a barely noticeable trail of blood droplets through the corridor to the door of the girl's room. She looked around. No one was in sight. Softly, she knocked. "Hello?" she whispered.

Sarah put her ear to the door and listened closely. She heard someone crying quietly inside the room. She let herself in.

The room was dark and lined on both sides with sleeping girls in beds—three on the right and two more on the left. In the bed closest to the door, a figure under the covers moved. Sarah placed her hand gently on the blanket-covered shoulder of the sad young girl. The girl turned to see Sarah's sweet, comforting face.

Careful not to wake the other girls, Sarah asked, "Can I help?"

The girl sniffled. "Who are you?"

"I am the new teacher. My name is Sarah." Sarah sat on the bed next to the girl. She felt something wet.

"Do you mind if I ask how old you are?" she asked.

"I'm the youngest one here. We just had a party for my fourteenth birthday," the girl answered with a hint of a smile as if she were recalling the happy celebration.

"It looks as if a child has become a woman." Sarah congratulated her, "*Mazel Tov!*"

Sarah's enthusiasm elicited a whimper.

"This is a happy occasion, not an unfortunate one, daughter of Jacob," Sarah continued. "What is your name?"

Embarrassed, the girl hesitated. "Chaya," she finally admitted.

"Well, Chaya, how about we get washed up?"

Chaya blushed in agreement.

"While you're in the lavatory, I'll change your sheets. Meet you there in a few minutes," Sarah instructed.

With Chaya headed for the washroom, Sarah secured new sheets from the linen closet and efficiently changed the bed in the dark room. Returning to the hallway, she scoured the supply closet for sanitary items, then met Chaya, as promised, in the washroom, where the new teacher taught her wary pupil what to do.

Soon, Chaya, clean and content, slipped back into bed, and Sarah covered her lovingly. The other girls in the room continued sleeping soundly.

Sarah leaned over and gave the girl a maternal kiss on her cheek. "Good night, Chaya," she whispered.

As Sarah turned to leave, Chaya latched onto the sleeve of Sarah's robe and tugged on her arm. "One more minute?" she requested.

Sarah smiled sympathetically. "One more minute," she agreed as she lay down next to Chaya, keeping the child company until she was fast asleep.

# Chapter 10

SEPTEMBER 29, 1938

Sanitized steel double doors burst open inside a small hospital in the heart of Berlin.

Manfred raced into the corridor with Erich hot on his tail. They stopped briefly at the nurse's station. Erich seemed a bit out of breath; Manfred was fine.

"Joel, Regina Joel," Manfred queried.

Busy at the counter, preoccupied with her paperwork, the woman in white didn't bother to look up. "Upstairs and down the hall, Room 218."

Up a flight of stairs and through the empty hallway, Manfred and Erich made a beeline for Regina's room.

Regina, now 30, protector of hearth and home, was lying restlessly on the bed, in the throws of active labor. Her hair was soaked to her scalp, and she growled like a lioness.

The only other person in the room, their housekeeper and trusted confidant, Frau Tietze, hovered by

Regina's bedside. Tietze, 43, a simple, hardworking woman, wearing a small gold crucifix around her neck, was holding a basin of hot water and towels. She carefully placed a wet compress on Regina's forehead.

Manfred rushed to his wife's side. "Regina, darling, I am here."

Regina moaned.

"Ah, I'll be in the waiting room if you need me," Erich added sheepishly as he scurried away.

Manfred held his wife's hand and wiped her brow. He looked at Frau Tietze and complained, "Skeleton crew at the front desk and no one to check her vitals. How did we end up here? I thought we had arrangements at the main hospital."

"*Ja,* Herr Joel, we went there and were turned away," she answered. "When they saw your wife's identification card, they refused to help her. The chief administrator said they—"

She stopped abruptly.

"What? What did he say?" Manfred insisted.

Frau Tietze answered reluctantly, "He said they don't deliver 'rats.'" Seeing Manfred's blood begin to boil, she tried to finish delicately, "He told us to go to a *Tierarzt.*"

"A veterinarian, huh?!" Manfred was incensed.

Regina moaned louder. She was sweating profusely.

"The baby is almost here," Tietze announced.

Manfred panicked, "What should we do?"

"Welcome *dein Kind* to this world."

Just in time, the woman in white from the nurse's station walked into the room and put on a pair of sterile medical gloves.

As Regina began to pant, Manfred began to perspire.

A high-pitched scream pierced the sound barrier.

From the waiting room, Erich could hear Regina in the final stages of labor. He plopped himself down on a chair, under an imposing portrait of Hitler, and picked up the *Volkische Beobachter,* Germany's leading newspaper.

Erich perused the front page of the party-line publication. A sinisterly crafted cartoon depicted a Jewish octopus encircling the globe with its massive tentacles. Erich smirked. He was used to the daily barrage of Nazi propaganda.

A baby cried. Erich put down the paper and rushed back to Regina's room.

Manfred collapsed, exhausted, onto the bed next to a worn out Regina. Frau Tietze wrapped the baby in a blanket and handed the child to the new parents.

Manfred noticed Erich at the door. "It's a girl!" he joyfully announced as he wiped a tear from his eye.

Erich bounced into the room to get a closer look. The baby was beautiful. "*Mazel Tov!* Regina, she looks like you!" he noted.

Manfred looked adoringly at his wife. Regina was glowing. He nuzzled her. "Now, what should we name our precious daughter?" he asked.

Regina motioned to Frau Tietze. "In the drawer, the announcement," she murmured.

Manfred seemed perplexed.

"Announcement?"

Seeing how spent Regina was from childbirth, Frau Tietze offered up the explanation. "The midwife handed it to us when we checked in," she said. "The Nazis want you to choose from a list of state-approved names for newborn Jews."

"Nonsense!" Manfred hissed. "Hitler will not name our daughter!"

"But Manfred, it's the law," Erich stated.

Manfred's rage was building.

Regina repositioned the baby. "It's okay, dear," she assured him. "What did you have in mind?"

Frau Tietze retrieved the announcement from the drawer and handed it to Regina, then busied herself at the layette.

"I was thinking...Faigele," he said.

Nothing pleased Regina more than to make her beloved husband happy. "Little Bird," she said, translating from Yiddish. "I like it. That will be her Jewish name." Regina proceeded delicately. "And we will choose a German name from the list. I like the one that sounds the least Jewish. I feel that may be our safest option."

She showed him the decree. "You see that one?" She pointed to a name. "How do you feel about Tania? I think it's very pretty."

Manfred considered it. "Tania Joel...hmm...I can live with that. I guess." He rolled it off his tongue once or twice and decided, "Actually, I like it! Well, then it's done. Our daughter has a name and we won't be arrested over it." He shook his head.

Regina carefully handed the baby to her husband. Manfred gazed into the child's innocent eyes. "To the rest of the world, you will be Tania, and to us, little Faigele, with the hope that one day, my precious bird, you may fly away from this place and taste true freedom."

Regina was sleepy and worn out from her delivery. She dropped the announcement on the floor. The new family snuggled closely on the bed. The warmth and the happiness were contagious, and smiles flooded the room like early morning sunshine when the drapes are first parted.

# Chapter 11

*B*eth Jacob's headmistress looked a bit frazzled as she spoke on the phone in her small, uncluttered office. She flipped through a bunch of neatly typed papers.

"Another German? You sent me a replacement from Berlin?" she begged incredulously. The protest was about to begin with vigor. "With all due respect, Mr. Schenkolewski—"

Meir Schenkolewski, an elderly, learned gentleman with long, silky white hair, spoke on an antique telephone from his Italian mahogany desk in his well-appointed study in New York City.

"Don't worry, Madam Headmistress. She will be a very good teacher."

Yetta tried to break in. "But—"

Schenkolewski cut her off. "Trust me," he assured her. "After all, I *am* the secretary of the World Beth Jacob Movement."

Repositioning his tall, bony body in his big, cognac-colored leather chair, he rhetorically asked in the most soothing of tones, "Would I steer you wrong?"

Sarah entered a small meeting room. Seated around a long table were about a dozen women of all different shapes and sizes. Yetta sat at the head of the table. She stood as Sarah entered.

"Ah Sarah, good morning. We've been waiting for you to begin our seven o'clock meeting."

Sarah checked her watch. It was 6:55.

Through the walls, she could hear the girls beginning their morning prayers. *This is a prompt crowd,* she thought.

Yetta forged on with an introduction. "Ladies," she continued, "this is the newest addition to our staff, Miss Sarah. She will be filling the Torah teaching position vacated by Frau Wachs, who retired over the summer. We have high expectations that Miss Sarah will do well here at Beth Jacob. After all, she bears the same name as our dear departed founder, Sarah Schenirer, may her soul be bound up in the bond of eternal life."

"Amen," came the collective reply.

Sarah half smiled as she sat in the only empty chair. It seemed to Sarah that perhaps Yetta was mostly trying to convince herself of her new teacher's merits.

In German and Polish, the other teachers offered Sarah a cacophony of greetings as they gave her the once-over. "Hello, welcome, *willkommen, milo mi paniq poznac.* Pleased to meet you."

Yetta shuffled some papers. "Now then, let's go over some basic rules and procedures." She shot Sarah a look. "After all, each of us knows how imperative it is to stick to a rigid schedule. Discipline and devotion to God are the pillars of our beloved Beth Jacob society, and it is we, the teachers of the daughters of Israel, who have been entrusted to raise these children with pious integrity so that they may lay the foundation of righteousness among our nation and our people Israel."

Yetta was on a roll. "It is our hope that one day these young girls will be the future great matriarchs of our Jewish descendants and pass on the lessons of loving kindness and devotion to Torah."

Sarah attempted to decode the information placed in front of her. It was written in Polish.

Yetta deliberately pushed forward. "I spent a good portion of the summer creating these new teaching guides, so if you'll please turn to page one..."

They did.

"At six a.m., we rise, dress, pray, and review our lessons from the previous day. Seven forty-five, breakfast. Eight o'clock, first period..."

Sarah struggled to keep up. One of the teachers whispered something to another. They giggled quietly. Sarah caught the indiscretion but chose to ignore it. It was the first day of school, and she was determined to be well prepared for her classes, which were set to begin just a short time later that morning.

# Chapter 12

*T*he girls were all back from summer vacation and settling into their new school routines. Sarah's classroom was relatively drab and sparse, with just the basics: desks, chairs, and a blackboard.

The necessary books and pencils were methodically lined up on her desk, which sat in the front corner of the classroom by the window that overlooked the majestic Vistula River to the west. She was already in the room when the girls began to file in.

Sarah greeted each girl personally, "Welcome. Welcome."

Some girls rolled their eyes. Some giggled. Several whispered to each other.

Sosia, 18, a short, round girl walked in first. "Another German instructor?"

She was followed by her best friend, Pesia, 17, a tall, thin girl. "Should be interesting."

Wearing the finest clothes, Devorah, 22, attractive and privileged, from a wealthy German family, filed past Sarah next. "This must be a joke. I could have stayed in Deutschland for this!"

Sarah overheard the comments but continued to give each girl a warm greeting anyway.

Chaya entered the room and exuberantly claimed a seat in the front row. She was the only student who was genuinely happy to see Sarah. Finally, all of the girls were seated and settled and Sarah took the opportunity to introduce herself.

"Good morning and welcome back to school," Sarah began. "I hope you all had an enjoyable summer break. I know many of you attended camp in the Carpathians, and that must have been wonderful. I'm sure you have many treasured camp memories you'd like to share, and we'll make time for that later."

Blank stares. Sarah sucked in a deep breath.

"I am your new teacher, Miss Sarah, and I'm sure you've heard by now that I am from Berlin."

Sarah wrote her name and the word "German" on the blackboard.

While her back was still to the girls, she extracted a pair of googly-eyed glasses from her skirt pocket and secretly placed them on her face. The girls looked at each other impatiently. Suddenly, Sarah turned around wearing the funny glasses. The girls laughed surprisingly hard. Her lesson had begun.

"Since I was born and raised in Germany, everything I see and experience is through a German lens. These are my German lenses."

The girls continued to laugh. They were not sure where this was going, but they certainly were tickled.

Sarah pointed to Chaya. "You!" she charged. "Where are you from?"

Chaya was caught off guard. "Well, um, right here. I mean, I am from Poland."

"Is anyone else from Poland?" Sarah asked, already sure of the answer.

Most of the girls raised their hands.

"So, you girls see and experience everything through Polish lenses," she explained. "Right?"

Chaya raised her hand. "What exactly do you mean?" she asked respectfully.

"Good question, Chaya!" Sarah thought for a moment.

"What will you be having for lunch?" she asked her eager student.

"Pierogi," Chaya answered as she and the other girls giggled.

Chaya came from an ordinary middle-class family. Her father, a cap maker from Lodz, had secured scholarship money to be able to afford to send his only daughter to Beth Jacob. Pierogi was a staple for her.

"I will be having *Kreplach*!" Sarah announced cheerfully. "Will we be eating the same thing?"

"Uh, I guess so…"

The girls clamored. They got it.

"Is there anyone in the class from any place other than Poland?"

A couple of honey-haired girls called out, "Czechoslovakia."

"You learn through Czechoslovakian lenses," Sarah said.

"And we eat *Knedliky!*" they exclaimed. Everyone roared with laughter.

Sarah proceeded full-steam ahead. "Is there someone from any other place?"

Devorah, the oldest in the class, was being groomed to make the transition from student to teacher. So far, she was not impressed with the new instructor. She begrudgingly raised her hand.

Sarah was pleased to have her participation.

"What is your name, dear?" Sarah queried.

"Devorah. One day soon, I hope to be on that side of the desk."

Sarah knew this one would take time and nurturing. For now, she hoped to at least find some common ground. "Okay, Devorah, my student teacher. It's nice to meet you. I think I know where you are from."

"*Ja.* I am also from Germany. I get the point. I imagine that I see everything through a German lens."

"Just like me," Sarah concluded.

Devorah's tone was sarcastic. "Just like you," she confirmed.

Sarah forged on with her lesson. "I think you girls understand."

Sarah removed the funny glasses. "So, what bonds us together? What lens do we all have in common that allows us to see, learn, and feel in the same way?"

Sarah was charged up and hopeful.

The girls thought about it.

Chaya's eyes brightened. "A Jewish lens!" she called out excitedly.

"Exactly, Chaya!" Sarah was relieved. She had made her point. "Our culture, language, prayer, traditions,

Torah, living Jewishly...*this* is our common connection."

Sarah noticed Devorah gazing out the window.
"Devorah? Are you with us?"

"Yes. But soon, summer will be over and the long,
cold Polish winter will set in. It's a shame to waste a
warm, beautiful day inside the classroom. Who knows
how many more we have left?"

Sarah didn't need to think about it twice. "You're
absolutely right," she encouraged. "Everyone outside.
Now."

The girls hesitated. Initially restless, they now
seemed glued to their seats.

Sarah urged them, "Let's go."

# Chapter 13

*M*emel rolled his minivan up to #10 Stanislava Street. I was excited and felt honored to be on this hallowed ground, the spot where the Beth Jacob teachers imparted the wisdom of the sages and Beth Jacob girls soaked up every bit of it, the actual building where they lived and studied, the very same piece of land by the river where they prayed and discussed, laughed and argued, nourished their souls and their young minds. I had learned of the Beth Jacob legacy during my own preparation to become a religious school teacher. The thought of a progressive movement in which Jewish women educated other Jewish women, at a time when only men were expected to study Torah, fascinated me. Now, I couldn't wait to feel their presence.

One by one, Mike, Josh, Memel, and I stepped out of the vehicle and stood in front of the four-story, gray concrete building wedged between similar buildings. The shotgun style of it reminded me of a row home I had once lived in as a child growing up in Northeast Philadelphia. Only we were a long way from Northeast Philly. I had to admit, I felt a little let down. The building looked relatively new, for Europe, kind of sterile and not architecturally interesting at all. Certainly not the old-world charm I was expecting. Eventually, I noticed an ancient monastery that loomed to the right. Ah, I thought. That was more like it. The façade of the Beth Jacob school may have been disappointing, but the old monastery was clearly a testament of its time. If only this decaying street in Krakow could talk, I thought.

I peered over my shoulder at the tranquil Vistula River. It was wider than I'd envisioned. Probably deeper, too.

In front of me were tall, thin, twin oak doors inset with vertical clear glass squares. The portal to learning.

Above a first-floor window, which was oddly encased in relatively new white security bars, hung a large, shiny black commemorative plaque.

It read in Hebrew, English, and Polish:

THIS BUILDING, BUILT AND DEDICATED IN 1927, WAS THE HOME OF THE BETH JACOB TEACHERS' SEMINARY FOUNDED IN 1917 BY SARAH SCHENIRER. IT WAS HERE THAT THE DAUGHTERS OF ISRAEL, FROM MANY COR- NERS OF CENTRAL AND EASTERN EUROPE, CAME TO STUDY TORAH. A SPARK KINDLED IN KRAKOW GREW TO A FLAME THAT RADI- ATED THROUGHOUT POLAND AND ACROSS

THE OCEANS. THIS LIGHT OF TORAH CON-
TINUES TO ILLUMINATE THE HEARTS AND
MINDS OF JEWISH GIRLS THROUGHOUT
THE WORLD.

*Including this girl,* I thought. I had no words.

Mike and Josh were silent too. I believe they felt what I felt, or maybe they just sensed my awe and were respectful of the moment.

Suddenly, Memel interrupted the quiet sanctity of our visit. I guess he felt compelled to do his job. "So...this was it," he flatly announced. "The Beth Jacob School for Girls."

That did it. I was back in real time.

I peeked in through one of the glass windows embedded in the door and saw a small foyer, a corkboard with some advertisements pinned on it, a couple of interior doors, and a narrow flight of stairs.

"What is it now?" I wanted to know.

"Still a school...for children with, how do you call it?" He searched for the correct phrase. "Special needs."

Just then, the double doors burst open. We jumped back a few feet as a female teacher and a gaggle of students exited the building and made their way toward the river bank.

The instructor was speaking to her students in Polish. The children were all smiles, chatty and giggly.

As the preoccupied group passed by us, I imagined that this was the legendary Beth Jacob crew.

They seemed to morph before my very eyes.

# Chapter 14

*S*arah and the girls flooded out through the front doors of the school to the lovely garden on the bank of the Vistula River and rested on the grass by the water's edge to study. On this day, the river seemed placid.

Devorah had something on her mind. "Miss Sarah," she inquired, "when did you decide to become a teacher?"

Sarah was a bit surprised by the question. "Ah, well..." She thought about it. "My desire to learn and to teach goes back as far as I can remember..." The question catapulted Sarah back to a time at her childhood home.

*She was about 20 years old and studying at a small, square, pinewood kitchen table. Two much younger sisters, 11 and 5, ran and played actively throughout the tiny house. Another sister, 15, a more serious and mature girl, helped their mother cut vegetables by a deep sink basin.*

*Sarah's father, Yichiel, a man of sufficient means, pulled up a wooden stool. His eyes were smiling.*

*"Sarahlah," he began affectionately, "it's been decided that you should leave the books to your brothers and help Mama prepare for the Sabbath."*

*Sarah looked at her mother, who shrugged. When Yichiel started a sentence with "It's been decided," he usually meant by him.*

*Just then, Sarah's 11-year-old sister playfully stole one of her books.*

*"Hey!" Sarah scolded the thief, then turned her attention back to her father. "Papa," Sarah protested, "don't tell me you still think it's only important for Jewish boys to study Torah while girls are supposed to learn how to keep a Jewish home and raise a Jewish family!" She cringed. "That's an ancient theory, and considering we are known as the People of the Book, I believe I have a lot of catching up to do, no?"*

*Sarah's five-year-old sister returned her missing book with an elfish grin.*

*"Thank you," Sarah acknowledged as the two little ones flanked her to listen intently to the conversation.*

*"My oldest daughter," Yichiel explained, "all you need to know, you can learn from the Binding of Isaac. Both Abraham and Isaac were ready to make sacrifices in God's name."*

*"Abraham was willing to sacrifice his son, and Isaac was prepared to make the ultimate sacrifice, himself," Sarah stated. She waited. "Is that my lesson for today?"*

*The little ones settled happily on Sarah's lap. She closed her books and nuzzled them.*

*Yichiel smiled approvingly. "Yes, as long as our choices sanctify God's name, they will be right. Remember it always. Now, you and your sisters..." He tickled the younger ones, causing them to giggle with delight. "Get ready for the Sabbath meal."*

Suddenly, Devorah's voice snapped Sarah back to the here and now.

"I also always had a desire to learn and teach," she remarked.

"Seems we have something else in common, Devorah," Sarah noted.

Somewhat reluctantly, Devorah confirmed, "*Ja,* it seems we do."

"Miss Sarah, would you put the glasses back on?" Sosia asked.

"Do it," Pesia implored.

"Please?" Chaya begged.

Just as Sarah complied, a handsome courier rode by on his bicycle. He noticed her and smiled. Reflexively, she smiled back, forgetting for the moment that she was wearing the silly glasses.

When the realization hit, she rapidly peeled them off with considerably more than a modicum of embarrassment.

# Chapter 15

*A* man carrying a small package wrapped in brown paper rang the bell later that afternoon at the Beth Jacob School.

Mordechai was ruggedly good looking, with thick curly brown hair. In his late thirties, he was trim and clean shaven and had chocolate brown eyes.

Sarah answered the door. Their eyes met. She recognized him immediately. He was the fellow on the bicycle.

She was instantly attracted to him. The feeling was mutual.

"May I help you?" Sarah asked shyly.

Mordechai stumbled over his words. "I, uh, that is, I have a delivery of books for the headmistress."

He showed her the package. She reached for it, but he pulled it back playfully. "Of course, I'll need a signature, please."

Sarah was flushed. "Of course," she replied.

As Sarah signed for the package, Effie darted out the door.

"Effie! Come back in here right now!" she demanded.

The cat coiled behind Mordechai's legs. He meowed softly and darted back into the school.

Mordechai smiled. "Effie?" he pondered.

"It's short for Ephraim," Sarah explained. "He was a stray that followed me to the door on the night I arrived. He's been my companion and the girls' mascot ever since."

"Arrived? Then you must be the new teacher I heard about." Mordechai sounded excited.

Not one for gossip, Sarah was a little miffed. "What do you mean, heard about?"

"Krakow is not so big; news travels fast."

"And packages?" she challenged him. "Do they travel fast as well?"

"Fast as my legs will carry them," he assured her. He decided it was time for a formal introduction. "I am Mordechai, the courier. I have a reputation here in Krakow."

"A reputation?" Sarah remarked slyly.

Mordechai reached into his shirt pocket. "Everyone knows that if someone has something that someone else wants, Mordechai is the man to deliver it! For you." Mordechai pulled out a dog-eared business card and handed it to Sarah. Sarah was both captivated by his strong jaw line and charmed by his enterprising personality.

"If there is anything you ever need," he continued, "you can reach me at this number. Anything! It's nice to meet you, Miss..."

He checked her signature. "Sarah!"

Mordechai handed her the package.

"Nice to make your acquaintance, Mordechai, the courier," she replied.

Sarah began to close the door. Mordechai stopped it with his free hand and made one last attempt at conversation. "I once had an uncle Ephraim. He was, how do you say? A real pussycat!"

Sarah giggled.

Satisfied that he had made a connection with the new Beth Jacob teacher, Mordechai smiled broadly. "I'll be seeing you around," he confirmed.

Putting the emphasis on the word "seeing," Mordechai curled his fingers to indicate glasses around his eyes.

Sarah closed the door. She was completely mortified. Again.

# Chapter 16

*S*arah entered the school cafeteria. It was bustling with activity. She looked a bit confused as she double-checked her schedule. Yes, this was where she was supposed to be.

Girls with empty baskets were queuing up in what looked like mini assembly lines.

Teachers and older girls, including Devorah, at the head of the lines, were hard at work filling baskets with bread, jam, and a few assorted pieces of fresh fruit.

Sarah made her way to Yetta, who was busy sorting out medical supplies.

"*Tikkun Olam,*" the headmistress declared as she placed a small glass bottle of alcohol and a wad of cotton bandages in Frida's basket. Frida, 16, a smart-looking girl with glasses, smiled.

"*Tikkun Olam?*" Sarah repeated curiously.

Yetta nodded as she filled the next girl's basket. "You look like you're wondering what is going on here." She immediately put Sarah to work. Handing her a large box filled with several small egg cartons, the head-mistress instructed, "Eggs on top so they don't break."

Sarah dove right in, carefully placing the egg cartons in baskets. "Well yes, I, uh, was wondering—"

"Repairing the world, showing kindness, doing for others. Our Beth Jacob girls are woven from the fabric of *Mitzvoth,* God's commandments. It's part of what we do here," explained Yetta.

Sarah looked proudly around the room at the enormity of the undertaking. "How often?"

"As often as necessary."

"Doing good deeds for our fellow Jews?" Sarah asked.

"Doing good deeds for our fellows," Yetta clarified. "Whoever needs help at the moment. We don't discriminate. A person in need is a person in need. Jew, Pole, German, it's all the same to a Beth Jacob girl. In and around Krakow, as long as we can reach them by foot or by train, we're there to help."

Reaching the front of the line, Chaya approached Yetta and Sarah with her half-filled basket.

Yetta tucked some antibiotics inside Chaya's basket, and Sarah topped her off with a carton of eggs. "Making our world a better place, huh?" Sarah acknowledged, sending the happy girl on her way with a wink. "With s*hayna maidels,* pretty girls, like these, I don't know how we could miss."

Confident that Sarah was on board, Yetta barked, "Next!"

# Chapter 17

NOVEMBER 9, 1938

*M*anfred's strong hand knocked on the beautifully carved crescent-shaped oak door
inside the New Synagogue on Oranienburgerstrasse.
He remembered learning about this house of worship's
consecration on Rosh Hashanah, the Jewish New Year,
of 1866 and how it had always been a central part of
Jewish life in Berlin. Walking in for the first time a few
years earlier, he had reveled in the synagogue's magnificent Moorish structure, inspired by the Alhambra
in Granada, with its gilded domes and ornate interior.
It had become more than just a place for worship for
Manfred and some other 3,200 Jewish Berliners. It was
also a place for meeting, teaching, studying, and
socializing. Not so very long ago, Berlin's elite, including Albert Einstein, had worshiped inside its immense
sanctuary. Recently, however, since the inception of

the Nuremberg Laws, with many Jews feeling pressure to leave Germany, the congregation had dwindled.

After a moment, a deep yet elegant male voice from the other side of the door answered, "Come in."

Manfred entered the room and closed the door behind him. He was dressed in work clothes and carried an old wooden toolbox.

The chief Rabbi, Felix Luxembourgh, stout, in his sixties with a long, frizzy, white beard, was at his desk, tackling a mountain of paperwork. Leather-bound books filled the rabbi's study from wall to wall.

At the end of a long workday, Manfred was happy to see a friendly face. "*Shalom*, Rabbi. Thank you for meeting me so late."

"It's no problem, Manfred," replied the rabbi. "I know you *Klempnerinnen* keep all kinds of hours. A plumber can never know when a pipe is going to burst. Besides, I have lots to catch up on." Smiling, he pushed his papers aside. "Please, make yourself comfortable." The rabbi motioned for Manfred to sit in the oversized, Bordeaux-colored upholstered chair across from his desk.

Manfred complied and placed his heavy toolbox on the floor next to him. The chair was so welcoming he wondered how he'd ever get up.

"Now, if I recall, you are here to schedule a baby naming for that beautiful new child of yours, right?" The rabbi was good about remembering the life-cycle events of his congregants. "How are Regina and little Tania doing?"

"*Baruch Hashem*, thank God, they're both fine," Manfred assured him. "We were hoping to do it this *Shabbos.*"

"This *Shabbos* it is. I will call you to the Torah for an *Aliyah,* an honor, and we will tell the congregation the baby's Jewish name, which, by the way, is...?"

"Faigele."

"Ah, Faigele." The rabbi wrote the name down. "Meaning little bird. That is a lovely name. A very good choice."

"Thank you, Rabbi," Manfred replied. "Regina and I thought so."

Manfred shook the Rabbi's hand.

"Give my best to your lovely wife and a kiss to that precious baby, and we will see all of you on the Sabbath."

"See you then," Manfred confirmed as he pried himself out of the big comfy chair, grabbed his toolbox, and turned to leave. Rabbi Luxembourgh got up from his seat and rounded his desk to politely escort Manfred from his office.

As they approached the door, they heard a loud crash, then hooting and hollering coming from the other side. They rushed out into the lavish hallway and looked over the majestic balcony at the opulent sanctuary below.

Plain-clothed *Sturmabteilungen,* SA Stormtroopers, wielding lead pipes were breaking stained-glass windows, bashing furniture, unraveling and tearing up Torahs, and desecrating other holy ritual objects, including precious silver Torah pointers called *yads,* antique candelabra and spice boxes used for the special concluding *Havdalah* service of the Sabbath. They were tossing together prayer books and anything else combustible and setting the piles on fire. The *Ner*

*Tamid,* Eternal Flame, was knocked to the floor, its decorative crystal housing cracked into hundreds of splintered pieces. The Holy Ark was burning.

Unbeknownst to Manfred and the Rabbi, *Kristallnacht,* the Night of Broken Glass, had begun.

Manfred and the rabbi watched in horror as their beautiful house of worship was mercilessly being destroyed. They sped down the steps from the balcony to the sanctuary and began shouting at the SA.

"Stop! What are you doing!?" demanded the rabbi.

An SA thug with wild black eyes and wiry bronze hair grabbed hold of the rabbi and placed his thick hands around the rabbi's neck.

"Oh yeah, Jew, what are you going to do about it?" the thug challenged.

Manfred sneaked up behind the SA and gave him a one-two punch, knocking him out cold.

Manfred and the rabbi ran out a side door to the front of the building on Oranienburgerstrasse. To their alarm, they saw hordes of SA thugs repeating similar horrific crimes at shops and residences up and down the street. Windows were being smashed and some stores looted. The word *JUDE,* JEW, was being spray-painted on buildings. Well-dressed Jewish men were being beaten and rounded up for arrest.

"Manfred, hurry home to your family. Make sure they're safe. I'll call the police and try to save the synagogue," instructed the rabbi.

Manfred protested. He wanted to stay and fight. For him, a bell had rung. "But Rabbi—"

The Rabbi was firm. "Go!" he demanded as he re-entered the burning synagogue. Manfred hesitated.

Then, heeding the rabbi's order and particularly worried for his family's safety, he grasped his toolbox and raced down the street, past the chaos, toward home. In his work clothes, he managed to blend in with the crowd and escape unnoticed.

Rabbi Luxembourgh made his way back to an office on the first floor. He picked up the phone and dialed the police.

"Precinct Police Chief Wilhelm Krutzfeld, *bitte*. It's an emergency!"

Glass shattered. Fire crackled. Panic began to set in as he waited to be connected.

"Krutzfeld! The synagogue is burning! Please come! We need your help! *Hilf!*" he pleaded.

A filthy finger depressed the receiver, terminating the call. The rabbi looked up to find another SA thug with a frenzied look in his eyes standing over him, ominously waving a long lead pipe.

"Hello, Rabbi. *Gute Nacht!*"

The thug raised the pipe over the rabbi's head.

Precinct Police Chief Wilhelm Krutzfeld had fair hair, a small pointed Aryan nose, and a slight build. In his early 40s, he was a family man who took his job very seriously.

He charged in through the impressive main entry doors with a handful of uniformed police officers.

"Halt! I demand you stop this immediately!" he ordered.

The thugs continued their mayhem. "We have orders to burn it down to the ground and all the other ones like it," one of them retorted. "It's the beginning of the end for Jews in the Fatherland! *Heil* Hitler!" He saluted.

Krutzfeld did not respond in kind. "Well, I am the chief of police of this district, and I order you to cease and desist immediately!" He pulled out a pistol from his holster and raised it in the air. He had their attention. "I will use this if I have to. Now, I am in charge here, and you all are done. Finished, you understand? Every one of you, out. Now! *Raus!*"

The marauding thugs filed out of the synagogue, taking their pipes and sledgehammers with them. Krutzfeld addressed his officers. "I'll call the fire department, but do what you can to put out these flames until they get here."

The officers gathered buckets from maintenance closets, filled them with water from a couple of large basins in the synagogue's kitchen, and began to douse the flames as Krutzfeld entered the downstairs office, looking for a phone. He spotted the rabbi lying unconscious on the floor. There was a pool of blood around his head. The telephone receiver was still in his hand.

"Rabbi!" Krutzfeld raced to the rabbi and cradled his head. He pressed the button on the phone to get a dial tone. He dialed quickly.

"*Ja,* this is Precinct Police Chief Krutzfeld. I need a company down here at the New Synagogue on Oranienburgerstrasse right away!" He paused to listen. "I don't care that you have orders from der Fuehrer to let them burn; you have orders from *me* to get over here and put it out! Now do it, before I come over there and start shooting. I've just finished loading my gun."

He looked down at the bloody servant of God in his arms.

Rabbi Luxembourgh moaned.

"And send an ambulance too. Quickly! *Schnell!*"

# Chapter 18

*T*here was a wall of glass that separated tourists from what remained of the New Synagogue's once magnificent sanctuary.

Under their Kelly-green satin yarmulkes, Mike and Josh stared at the crumbled reminder of the beauty and sanctity that once was. There was no more balcony, no sign of the comfortable permanent seating, no *bimah*, platform, to stand on while leading services, no Holy Ark to house the Torah. Nothing remained but a wide space, open to the elements, filled with rubble, unsupported by a surviving partial stone pillar or two.

Soon, Josh noticed that various other male tourists, milling around and speaking a range of hushed multilingual tones, were wearing identical green skullcaps.

Confused, Josh double-checked the inside of his yarmulke. It read, "Josh Whitman's Bar Mitzvah, June 25, 2005."

"What's going on?" he asked his dad.

Mike took notice of the sudden plethora of identical green yarmulkes. He laughed. "Mom donated the left-overs on her way in."

Josh seemed relieved and a little bit proud all at once.

I playfully prodded the boys with a thick paperback book. "Look at what I found!" I chortled, flashing the sizable softcover before them, clearly unable to contain my zeal.

Mike examined the cover. "Jews in Kreuzberg," he read. "Where did you find that?"

"Gift shop," I retorted.

An avid reader, Josh excitedly grabbed the book and speedily flipped through it. He looked somewhat disappointed. "It's all in German," he announced. "How are you gonna read this?"

"I don't need to *read* it," I said flatly. "Look at page 27."

Josh turned to page 27, and I pointed to a couple of lines a little over two-thirds of the way down.

"There! My research has paid off."

Mike read silently over Josh's shoulder. Father and son were stunned.

"Check it out," I continued as I slid my finger across the page.

"One forty-four Oranienstrasse."

"Oh my God!" Mike shrieked.

"Their Berlin address!" Josh exclaimed.

I squealed with delight as I carefully reclaimed my prized find. "Yep!"

Ever mindful of our full itinerary, I asked the boys if they were ready to move on. "What do you say we have a look around upstairs?"

They agreed.

As we headed toward a winding white staircase with black metal rails, we passed an old framed 8x10 photo hanging on the lobby wall.  It caught my eye.  Behind the non-glare glass was a picture of a very Aryan looking policeman, fortyish, with fair hair and a small pointed nose.

Mike and Josh started up the stairs while I stopped to read the caption.  In a bold black font, it gratefully acknowledged and briefly told the story of one very brave Captain Wilhelm Krutzfeld.

# Chapter 19

SPRING, 1939

*I*t was a beautiful early afternoon in Krakow. Chirping birds seemed to be singing a welcome song to the first warm, sunny day of the new season. The serenity of the Vistula River was mirrored by the peaceful, quiet lesson being taught by Sarah on its greening bank.

"The rabbis tell us that in order for a day to be considered and counted as a day of life, it must be filled with Torah and good deeds," she related to an exceptionally attentive group of students.

"A day of eating, sleeping, and small talk is a day of mere existence," Devorah contributed. Devorah's teaching skills were becoming progressively more mature.

"We must strive to make each day count as a day of life!" Chaya chimed in. Chaya was always joyfully engaged in Sarah's company. She was a shining star.

Unexpectedly, Mordechai rode up to the girls on his beat-up old bicycle. He was carrying a package so cumbersome that he almost dropped it when he hit the brakes. The girls politely pretended not to notice. His near miss only served to endear him even more to Sarah, who was pleased as punch to see him again. "Delivery?" she asked in a cordial manner so as not to be too obviously interested.

"For Devorah," he answered with an enticing smile. "I'll take it in; it's rather heavy," he offered.

Sarah was impressed with Mordechai's understated chivalry. "Upstairs, first dorm room on the left."

"Thank you, Mr. Mordechai," Devorah graciously responded.

Finding it nearly impossible to resist, the other girls imitated Devorah in their silliest of voices. "Thank you, Mr. Mordechai!" they teased in unison.

The girls erupted in giggles.

Sarah and Mordechai exchanged a parting glance. She blushed. This time, Sarah thought, it looked as if he did a little bit, too.

The commotion outside attracted the attention of Yetta, who was drowning in paperwork at her normally tidy desk in her clutter-free second-floor office.

Feverishly annoyed, she darted a look out the window and saw Sarah sharing a laugh or two with her young charges.

Yetta mumbled something under her breath before promptly drawing the heavy brown curtains.

# Chapter 20

*O*ur journey would be filled with small victories and defeats, but on this particular day, we had to chalk up one huge disappointment.

Mike, Josh, and I stumbled out of Rolf's car onto Berlin's busy Oranienstrasse. Rolf led us to what appeared to be a used-car lot surrounded by a cyclone fence. He looked confused as he double-checked a cross section of a map. We surveyed the area.

I grabbed the fence with both hands and flung my body against it. "What the hell is this?" I demanded.

Rolf walked a few yards and examined the address on the nearest building. He returned with an apologetic look on his ever-softening face. "That one is one forty-one to one forty-two, which means one forty-three to one forty-four should be right here," he said regretfully. "I suppose the building didn't survive the war."

Staring wistfully through the fence, we could only imagine the pre-war stone architecture that had once occupied this now long-forgotten, severely neglected piece of ground.

# Chapter 21

*I*t was just another typical mid-afternoon in the adequately cozy Joel flat at number one forty-four Oranienstrasse.

Six-month-old Tania was happily chattering to herself on the floor as she played with a brand-new doll. Albeit a bit stiff, the wooden playmate had prettily painted short orange hair and an adorable scrunched face with pursed pale-pink lips. Tania was enchanted.

Frau Tietze was at the stove, transferring hot chicken noodle soup from a tall cast-iron pot to a large sculpted ceramic serving dish. As she poured, the aroma filled the home; even the neighbors could pick up the scent of wafting fresh dill.

At the small dining room table, Regina and Manfred, who was home from work for lunch, listened to the radio. It broadcast a fiery political speech by Propaganda Minister Josef Goebbels.

"The noose is tightening around the necks of German Jews," Manfred declared stoically.

Regina glanced at her daughter, who continued playing contentedly, unaware of the harsh realities consuming her world. She tried to subdue her fear. "Do we wait it out, or should we go?" she asked worriedly.

"It will be difficult to get papers," Manfred responded. "But if we stay," he continued, "who will help us?"

Regina reached for her husband's hand. "Who can we trust?" she thought out loud.

Frau Tietze placed the steaming tureen of hot soup on the table in front of them. "Me," she declared emphatically.

Surprised, Regina and Manfred looked up at her. Through a savory scented chicken and noodle infused mist they could see her sweet, comforting smile. Frau Tietze assured them, "You can trust me."

# Chapter 22

*T*he Beth Jacob girls were wrapping up their the-
atrical retelling of the story of Purim on a
makeshift stage in the school cafeteria. The play
chronicled a time in Persian history when the Jewish
Queen Esther rescued her people from certain annihilation at the hands of an evil man called Haman. Students and staff alike were enjoying the traditional
merriment and revelry of the holiday, which included
homemade costumes for the players and an abun-
dance of wine for the adults.

The teachers were a cheerfully supportive audience.
Meir Schenkolewski was in attendance. Beaming like
a proud grandfather, he occupied a reserved seat in
the front row.

Devorah strummed a guitar on the side of the stage
for dramatic effect.

Sosia, dressed as an old Jewish man in a yarmulke and
robe, using a large branch that had fallen from one of the
trees along the river as her cane, and bearing a name tag

that read, "Uncle Mordecai," recited her last line. "Esther, you should be proud of yourself. You have saved your people!"

Chaya made a lovely queen. Wrapped from head to toe in recycled regalia, complete with an aluminum crown and a broom-handle scepter, she took a graceful bow.

The teachers burst into a standing ovation as the rest of the girls joined Sosia and Chaya to revel in the accolades.

Sarah rushed the stage. She congratulated each girl individually on a fine performance. The girls kissed and hugged her.

Chaya tugged on Sarah's shoulder and whispered in her ear, "May we call you Mother Sarah?"

Sarah was flattered. "Well, yes, of course. I would like that very much."

From the other side of the room, Yetta and a homely-looking heavy-set Jewish ethics teacher with a pleasant disposition, Miss Aviva Gorski, looked on curiously.

"Why do you think the girls respond to her so?" Yetta wondered aloud. Aviva shrugged in awe.

Approaching the women from behind, Schenkolewski overheard. "Because she respects and empowers them," he explained. "She truly loves them, and they know it. They respond to her because the feeling is mutual. They are returning the love."

As Aviva and Yetta shrank away in embarrassment, Schenkolewski made his way toward Sarah and the girls.

Chaya enthusiastically leaped in front of the others to greet him. "Thank you for being here, Mr. Schenkolewski," she gushed. "We look forward to your visits!"

The other girls agreed.

"It is my pleasure," he assured them. "God didn't bless me with grandchildren. You, my dear girls, are it!"

Chaya threw her arms around him.

"I must return to America tomorrow," he continued. "But if any of you ever need anything, you know how to reach me."

The girls confirmed with nods and smiles.

"Thank you again for the recommendation," Sarah whispered in his ear.

Schenkolewski winked at Sarah. He glanced back at Yetta. As usual, she was scowling.

"Say no more," he chuckled. "You're welcome. Please give my regards to your family."

Sarah nodded before leading the girls in the blessing over the fruit of the vine.

"*Boray p'ree hagafen,*" Sarah jubilantly recited.

The girls raised their cups of juice and drank. Sarah and Schenkolewski treated themselves to a bit of sweet elderberry wine and an unspoken toast.

# Chapter 23

*Y*etta flipped through a picture book on Palestine as she strolled through the dormitory hallway one late afternoon. Photos of Jewish pioneers planting date trees, irrigating arid soil, and building infrastructure, roads, railroads, and schools filled every page.

It was free time for the girls—a time to wash, rest, get caught up on letter-writing to families, and prepare for supper.

As she passed Devorah's room, Yetta detected an unfamiliar noise coming through the thin walls. She pressed her ear against the closed door. Yetta was expecting to hear the soft, sweet strumming of Devorah practicing on her guitar, but instead, she was horrified to recognize the frightening shrill of an angry German voice.

She burst in.

Gathered around the bed, Devorah and a handful of other girls were listening to a shortwave radio. They were so engrossed in the activity that none of them noticed when Yetta entered the room.

Adolph Hitler's voice echoed from the speakers. *"Juden sind hier nicht erwunscht!"*

Devorah translated. "Any Polish Jew living in Germany must leave immediately. Jews are not welcome here."

Yetta interrupted as Hitler's voice droned on. Her eyes were wide and fearful. "Where did you get the radio?" she demanded.

Startled, Devorah quickly turned it off.

The girls didn't answer.

"I asked you a question." Yetta persisted. "Beth Jacob rules strictly forbid being in possession of such an item on school grounds. Now where did you get it?"

Devorah fessed up. "My father sent it in his last care package from Germany, madam. He thought it would be helpful for me to keep track of what is going on back home." She hesitated, then admitted, "But it all sounds a bit scary."

Yetta was fuming. "Precisely why we don't need a radio," she exclaimed. "I don't want you girls getting upset over Nazi propaganda. It's just the rants and ravings of a crazed lunatic."

Nonetheless, Devorah was deeply concerned. "Madam Headmistress, I think Jews are being arrested and chased from their homes in Germany."

"We are not in Germany," Yetta clarified sternly. "We are in Poland. This does not affect us."

The girls weren't certain whom their headmistress was trying harder to convince, them or herself.

"My parents and my little brother..." Devorah persisted.

"I'm quite sure your family can take care of themselves," Yetta insisted. "You girls need only to be concerned with Torah and prayer. That's what your parents are paying tuition for. I think they'd agree that you should concentrate on your studies."

"But—"

"Devorah, hand over the radio! Now!"

Suddenly, the sweet and calm voice of Sarah interrupted the mounting melee. "May I?"

Devorah, Yetta, and the rest of the girls turned around to see Sarah leaning against the doorjamb. Her left arm was outstretched.

Sarah knew Yetta, in her own misguided way, was only trying to protect the girls. "I'll take the radio for safe-keeping. That is, if you don't mind, Madam Headmistress."

Yetta huffed. "Fine. Devorah, please hand over your radio to Miss Sarah. I'll see all of you in the dining hall for the prayer service before the meal in exactly one half hour." She stormed out, giving a discerning look to both Sarah and the girls before leaving.

Devorah reluctantly relinquished her radio to Sarah. "Is it true, what she says, Miss Sarah? That we don't have to worry," she asked.

Sarah could see that the girls were looking to her for reassurance. "Let's leave the radio and the worrying to the grown-ups. Don't forget, there is an entire Polish army between us and the Nazi party. Devorah," she continued, "after dinner, we will try to contact your family to make sure they are all right and put your mind at ease. Okay?" Sarah gave Devorah a wink.

Devorah nodded. "Yes, *Mother* Sarah," she replied.

This was the first time Devorah had called her teacher Mother Sarah, and there wasn't a soul in the room who didn't notice. Sarah was pleased. The rest of the girls felt comforted. Many of them sighed in relief.

"Now, go wash up," Sarah instructed. "I'll keep an ear on the radio, and if there is anything you girls need to know, I will tell you."

"Promise?" Chaya begged.

"Promise," Sarah confirmed.

The girls ran out of the room. Sarah looked down at the radio in her arms and then up toward heaven. The warm, reassuring smile that she always wore around the girls was beginning to fade. "I'm going to need a little strength," she uttered. Her words were barely audible.

# Chapter 24

The next morning, Effie purred contentedly as he lapped up a bit of milk from a shallow stone bowl on the floor.

A group of girls including Chaya, Frida, and Hannah, 15, fair and freckled, were eating breakfast together. Devorah sat alone. There was a plate of food in front of her with two eggs, softly poached, and a slice of rye bread, lightly toasted. But she wasn't eating.

Sarah, dining at the staff table, kept a worried eye on Devorah.

"Did anyone hear what happened last night when Devorah tried to reach her family?" Chaya anxiously asked. "Was she able to contact her parents and little brother in Germany?"

"I heard she spoke briefly to her mother, who told her they were going into hiding," Frida answered.

"Hiding?" Pesia wondered aloud.

"From the Nazis," Frida clarified.

"What does that mean? How will she find them if they are hiding? What if she can't? Will she ever see them again?" Chaya had so many questions.

Unfortunately, there were no answers. Frida and Pesia shrugged their shoulders. Chaya stared pitifully at Devorah, who had a veil of despair cloaking her pretty face.

The girls watched as Sarah approached Devorah and placed her loving arms around her.

Sarah and Devorah spoke privately.

The girls felt badly for their friend, and powerless and helpless. A wave of depression swelled over each and every one of them.

Reality was creeping ever closer to home.

# Chapter 25

"Wrench!" Manfred cheerfully called out from under the kitchen sink. Lying on his back, he attempted to adjust a leaking pipe.

Seated on the floor by his mentor's work boots, Erich was at the ready with the appropriate tool at the appropriate time. He handed Manfred a torque wrench.

At the table, Regina happily tended to her motherly duties and fed warm cereal to her nearly one-year-old daughter.

Frau Tietze busied herself with household chores.

This morning at the Joel residence was calm and peaceful until, unexpectedly, the buzzer sounded.

"Manfred, Erich, in the back," Regina ordered with alarm in her voice. "Frau Tietze, the door."

The family sprang into action. Manfred and Erich darted into the bedroom. Regina lifted the baby from her high chair and held her closely in her arms.

Frau Tietze cautiously approached the door and looked at Regina before proceeding. Regina nodded the go-ahead, and Tietze opened the door a crack, keeping the security chain safely engaged.

"*Guten Tag!*" came a hearty, friendly sounding woman's voice from the hall.

Tietze closed the door and looked back at Regina. She seemed relieved. "It's your sister and her son."

"Hurry, let them in," Regina responded. "Manfred! It's Rosa *und* Josef," she bellowed toward the rear of the flat.

Manfred and Erich emerged from the back room as Tietze welcomed the visitors into the apartment. Regina placed Tania back in the high chair to continue her feeding.

Rosa Tymberg, Regina's older sister, was a full-figured, eternal optimist in her late thirties. She was a proud German who never considered herself anything else. Her husband, Samuel, had died in 1930 from an incurable illness. Her only child, Josef, at age ten, was a shy yet very polite, well-mannered boy.

"Thank you, Frau Tietze," Rosa acknowledged in a familiar way as she entered the flat.

Tietze smiled and led them to the kitchen, where she picked up a hand towel and began drying some dishes that had been resting in a wooden dish rack.

Regina wrapped her arms around Rosa and gave her a big, warm hug. Then she kissed her reserved, skinny nephew on the forehead.

Manfred offered Rosa a kiss on each cheek and playfully tussled Josef's brown hair before he and Erich returned their attentions to the underbelly of the sink.

"Rosa, little Josef, what a nice surprise!" Regina was always delighted to spend time with family.

"Sorry to come unannounced," Rosa apologized.

"So, what brings you here today, my darling sister?" asked Regina as she scooped some cereal off the side of Tania's upper lip. Little Tania squealed with delight. "You should have told me you were coming. I would have made a meal."

"No time for that," Rosa replied abruptly. Her mood was palpably somber. "I brought Josef to say good-bye."

Regina stopped feeding the baby. Manfred surfaced from under the sink. Frau Tietze put down the towel. Erich quietly placed a pipe fitting back into the toolbox.

"Good-bye?" Regina asked incredulously. "What do you mean? Where is he going?"

"I am putting him on a *Kindertransport* to Belgium. From there, he'll take a boat to Harwich, England, where our sister Hanni will pick him up. She'll take him back to London with her and care for him there until this Hitler nightmare is over, at which time, God willing, we will be reunited."

"How did you accomplish this?" Manfred wanted to know.

"I registered him as an orphan at the Jewish orphanage."

He commended her, "Rosa, I admire your tenacity. Of everyone in the family, you are truly the organizer."

Regina was dismayed. "But that's so extreme," she exclaimed. "Frau Tietze has offered to help us. Perhaps—"

"I'll make a call," Frau Tietze interjected. She began to move toward the phone.

Rosa stopped her. "It's been decided," she insisted.

"Do you really think it's necessary to ship the poor child to Britain all by himself?" Regina asked.

"He won't be alone," Rosa explained. "He'll be with thousands of other Jewish children. I must have faith in this journey, Regina. I have no other choice. Things are getting much worse for German Jews."

"It's true, Regina," added Manfred. "We've already been ordered to relinquish our valuables to the city pawnbroker."

Manfred remembered feeling virtually handcuffed after surrendering the family's gold and silver pieces as he then watched town hall authorities demand his wife's wedding ring as well. He had managed to keep his left hand in his coat pocket throughout the ordeal.

"And now we are subject to a Jewish Council," he continued.

Erich chimed in. "Next, I heard they are considering making us wear a yellow star on our clothing, some type of Jew badge."

Erich recalled walking past the old textile factory. Peering in the window, he had seen sheets of yellow fabric rolling off the presses, with broken black outlines of Jewish stars and the word *Jude* printed on them.

Josef tickled the baby. He gently wrangled the spoon from his *Tante*, Aunt, Regina's momentarily paralyzed hand and took over her feeding.

Rosa looked sadly but lovingly at her boy. "He leaves today."

Regina and Manfred were aghast. "Today!?" they blurted in unison.

"In one hour. His bags are downstairs." Rosa directed her son, "Josef, say good-bye to your family."

Josef did as he was told. He hugged each one of them. He looked sad and remained quiet. He kissed the baby on her cheek. Then he ran to his mother's side and wept. She put her big arms around him and choked back her tears. "Good-bye then," she said. "Regina, I'll be in touch."

Regina called, "Manfred, get the baby's sweater! Rosa, we'll go with you and Josef to the train station."

"No, thank you," Rosa declined. "This is something between a mother and son. Please, let us go alone."

Manfred held Regina back.

She relented. "I understand. As you wish." Then Regina added sadly, "Good-bye, dear boy. God be with you."

Josef finally spoke. "See you again one day," he said resolutely.

Frau Tietze dropped a dish on the kitchen floor. It shattered.

A fierce look was born in her Aryan blue eyes.

# Chapter 26

The station was crowded and noisy as parents frantically boarded their children onto the trains. Nazi guards checked papers and barked out orders. The Nazis managed the task of getting children with rucksacks into the train cars with bats of their rubber truncheons or kicks from their polished boots.

Children of all ages were crying; parents wept. It was just the beginning of a difficult, traumatic separation and confusing journey for Josef Tymberg and some 10,000 other European Jewish children who would ultimately board the *Kindertransport* to safety.

"Don't forget to keep an eye on your belongings," Rosa told her son. "You'll need your jacket to keep you warm, and I packed some food to eat when you get hungry— your favorite biscuits and some meat. Keep your shoes on so they don't walk away without you. And here is some money in case you have an emergency. Okay?"

Rosa gave Josef a few bills, which he promptly stuffed into his coat pocket. He solemnly nodded an acknowledgment to his mother and offered her one last, lingering hug. His eyes welled up. She stayed strong.

"Smile, *Liebchen*. *Tante* Hanni will take good care of you. She will probably spoil you with sweets! God bless you and keep you safe, my son. We will see each other again. I promise."

Rosa kissed her son on each cheek and watched as he was one of the last children to board the train. She waved good-bye, and he responded in kind. A Nazi guard kicked him onto the train, hard.

"*Schnell!*" the Nazi shouted.

Rosa bit her tongue and tried her best not to react. Just a few more minutes and her little Josef would fade completely from view.

The doors closed, and the train whistled. Rosa could deny her feelings no longer. She turned her head away and burst into tears. As the train departed behind her, her chest began to heave.

Inside the train cars, Nazi guards strutted like proud peacocks up and down the aisles, looting the children, taking food and valuables from their rucksacks and fleecing their pockets for money.

Josef was not exempt. Within minutes of being seated on the train, he had been robbed by the Nazi who had kicked him onboard of everything that Rosa had sent with her son for his long, uncertain trek to London.

In the process of looting Josef, the Nazi found the meat, unwrapped it, and shoved it into his carnivorous mouth, devouring it in front of the children with a sadistic grin on his ugly face.

Josef quietly took it like a man.

# Chapter 27

*A*publication entitled *Growing the Beth Jacob Movement: Making the Jerusalem Dream a Reality* by Meir Schenkowlewski was in Sarah's delicate hands.

On this particular night, she found it extremely difficult to concentrate on her routine bedtime reading.

Closing the book abruptly, she removed her reading glasses and turned out the light on her small, rickety nightstand.

Allowing her head to fall gently back into the feather pillow, she tried desperately to sleep but only managed to participate in an endless marathon of first tossing, then turning.

Having an unsuccessful go at slumber, she turned the light back on, slipped out of bed, walked to her narrow closet, and retrieved Devorah's shortwave radio. She turned it on, quietly.

Static. Sarah fumbled with the tuning button until she found a broadcast frequency.

On the radio, Hitler ranted, "...the annihilation of the Jewish race in Europe!"

Enraged, Sarah threw the radio against the wall with such force that it broke into several pieces.

The Nazi beast was moving closer, she feared, and beginning to spread through Europe, like the plague that it was.

# Chapter 28

*T*he photographer's studio was set up in his airy apartment just a few floors above the Joel flat.

Regina, in a snug, dark dress with a decorative white collar, straightened Manfred's houndstooth tie.

"There. Very handsome!" she said admiringly.

Manfred smiled. He grabbed his wife enthusiastically and planted a passionate kiss on her full, dark red lips.

"Thank you, my love."

Regina giggled, playfully pushed her husband away, and turned her attention to Tania. She fussed with the right side of her daughter's baby-fine auburn hair. "I can't seem to get this one curve to behave."

Manfred cocked his head and checked out his wife's shapely bottom. "I see what you mean."

Immediately realizing what her husband was referring to, she chastised him.

"Manfred!"

Tania, in a cute little ensemble that mimicked her mother's, seemed oblivious to her parents' frisky behavior. She was busy primping her doll's hand-knitted attire for the photo.

Hans, the photographer, was the son of an old acquaintance and a longtime neighbor. In his early twenties, he was affable and professional as he entered the room. "All right then, are we ready?" he asked.

Regina gave up on the misbehaving hair curl. "Oh well, that'll just have to do. Come on, Tania, let's take a picture *mit Vati,* with Daddy."

Tania took her mother's hand and followed her to the monochrome floral backdrop where her father awaited. Manfred whispered into Regina's ear. "Are you happy that you are finally getting your family portrait?"

"Thank you, darling," Regina said with a smile. "You know how much this means to me. No matter what happens to us, to our family, we'll always have this one last perfect moment."

Manfred put his strong, loving arms around his family and kissed both of his girls on their cheeks.

Hans took the opportunity to position them in size order, starting with Tania and her doll on the left. He stepped behind the tripod and looked through the lens of his camera.

"Squeeze in tight, please."

Manfred leaned in closer to his wife. Tania grew impatient and squirmed. Regina held her daughter firmly in place.

"Right, that's it. *Gut!*"

FLASH!

The Joel Family was immortalized on film for eternity.

# Chapter 29

*I*n the middle of the night, Regina was awakened by the incessant ringing of the telephone.

She glanced at Manfred sleeping in the bed next to her. He stirred.

Worried that the sound might soon wake their daughter, Regina popped up, threw on her pink silk bath robe, and hurried to the parlor.

She answered the call anxiously, "*Hallo.*"

Half awake and trying to give his eyes time to adjust, Manfred joined his wife in the parlor. He didn't feel the need to be overly concerned until he noticed that her hands were shaking.

Regina placed the receiver down and turned to her husband. The anguished look in her eyes confirmed that something was terribly wrong.

"We have to go," she said.

# Chapter 30

SEPTEMBER 1939

BLITZKRIEG

HITLER INVADES POLAND

POLISH ARMY FOLDS

*B*right, colorful student artwork adorned the walls of Sarah's classroom, and the desks were covered with wide-open notebooks. Pencils toiled furiously. It was business as usual.

Today, Sarah was teaching the girls a bit of conversational Hebrew, just in case any of them should ever make it to Palestine.

Without warning, the lesson was interrupted.

Yetta barged into the classroom. Her face was beet red, and she was so out of breath, she could barely speak.

Sarah could only speculate on the cause of this interruption. Instead, she confronted Yetta directly. "Madam Headmistress, what is it?"

"Sarah..." Yetta flashed an official Nazi document.

Sarah stopped her. "Maybe we should discuss this in the hallway," she said, looking at her students' disturbed faces.

"No!" several of their voices protested.

Deborah spoke for the group. "It's probably something that is going to affect us anyway," she stated. "If you don't mind, we'd prefer to hear it sooner rather than later."

"I suppose you are right," Sarah considered. "Please continue, Madam Headmistress. What is it?"

The girls braced themselves.

"It's an announcement," Yetta declared. "From the Germans. About armbands and—"

Sarah cut to the chase. "What does it say?"

Yetta took a moment to choke down some air. Then she summarized the decree. "Jews cannot use public transportation without permits; we must stay on certain streets until curfew; we cannot even sit in the park or we'll be arrested. All Jewish shops, offices, apartments, and establishments must be marked as Jewish with a Star of David, and—"

Sarah was in shock. "There's more?"

Yetta's tears began to flow. She could barely finish. "Every Jewish school must close its doors immediately."

The girls gasped. Some of them cried out.

Sarah wasted no time on sorrow. She got angry. "Girls, the Nazis may be able to empty our beloved building of students and books, but they will *never* empty our minds of Jewish learning. Whoever can be reunited with their families will be, and the rest of us will find a way to stay together."

Her resolve was unshakable.

# Chapter 31

The Krakow train station was a mob scene.

Hundreds of people with packed bags were standing and sitting, waiting for passage out of town. Most people were headed east, trying to flee the approaching Germans. Some were just trying to reunite with family members in other nearby towns. Children were crying, parents were screaming and arguing, families with all of their belongings were struggling to stay together.

It was close to 3:00 p.m. when Sarah, Miss Aviva, and about a dozen girls arrived at the depot.

They huddled together and tried to make the best of the congested situation while joining too many people waiting for too few trains.

"What about you?" Aviva asked Sarah.

"I will care for the remaining girls."

"Maybe I should stay and help."

"Absolutely not," Sarah responded. "All of the Beth Jacob teachers were able to locate their families. Families must be reunited. That includes yours."

"And *your* family?" Aviva asked. "What about them?"

"I could never leave any of the girls alone. My family will understand."

Finally, running somewhat behind schedule, a train arrived, stopping at the station. It was already completely full. People squeezed anyway into the cramped cars.

Aviva hesitated.

"But there are still so many to look after..."

"I'll figure it out," Sarah said. "Now get on the train. I insist."

Reluctantly, Miss Aviva hopped on first. Then she and Sarah made room for the girls. All but the smallest one, Bracha, managed to get on.

Sarah spotted an open window. "Here, Bracha, through the window!"

Sarah hoisted her young student up, grabbed hold of her surprisingly broad bottom, and shoved her through the window. Aviva secured her from the other side. Sarah pushed Bracha's bag through the window too.

"Good-bye, my friend and dear students," Sarah called. "Find your families and your way to safety. God be with you."

Bracha stuck her head back out through the window. She looked concerned. "How many of us are left?" she beseeched.

The train whistle blew. Sarah lifted her response over the cacophonous noise. "Ninety-four."

The train started to depart. Aviva and the girls waved sadly.

"I'll say a blessing for you," Sarah shouted as the train chugged down the tracks.

"Mother Sarah, you *are* the blessing," Bracha shouted back.

Sarah managed a faint smile to alleviate their worries as she waved them good-bye.

Leaning out doors and windows to get one last look at their devoted colleague and teacher, Miss Aviva the girls noticed that Sarah appeared to get smaller and smaller as the train picked up speed until eventually, she disappeared entirely from their view.

# Chapter 32

*I* remembered reading online about the old Jewish district of Krakow, known as Kazimierz. It was liquidated by the Nazis in March, 1941. All Jews were marched over the nearby Powstancow Slaskich Bridge straight into the ghetto. Little did they know, most of them would never cross that bridge again. The thought haunted me as Memel pulled his van up next to a six-foot-tall monument in an open empty field. A few large rocks led up to the structure, and both flowers and pebbles adorned the stone.

"As you can see, there is nothing left of the Plashow Concentration Camp," he pointed out.

Memel continued driving. He needed to show us something a little further down the road.

"Over there on your right."

He slowed to a near stop so we could get a good look.

"See that house? That was Amon Goeth's villa. He was the monster that ran the camp."

We couldn't believe what we saw. On the front gate, spray-painted in sizable dark-blue letters, were the words "NO KIKES."

From our seats, Mike and I shook our heads in disgust.

Josh rolled down his window and flipped the bird.

Our guide hit the gas and drove on, over the bridge and into Kazimierz.

Memel then led us to the small Jewish cemetery encased in a waist-high black wrought-iron fence adorned with menorahs on every panel. The cemetery was situated just inside the large square of what used to be the thriving Jewish quarter. The square itself was framed all the way around by a few magnificent but mostly defunct synagogues, like the Alte (Old) Synagogue, which dated back to the end of the 15th century and housed a precious collection of ancient Judaica. The nearby Remu Synagogue, built in 1558 with its beautifully arched welcoming doors, Memel informed us, was the only synagogue left in Krakow where Jews—a handful of surviving Polish Jews, but mostly tourists—could still attend a worship service. The larger synagogues of Poland, he told us, the ones with high, grand entrances, had been used by the Nazis as horse stables. The occupiers had placed troughs on the *bimahs* and found it especially entertaining when their animals defecated on the sacred areas that housed the Holy Arks. It was no coincidence that in cities all over Poland, Nazis had sent Jews to live in overcrowded, unsanitary horse stables at concentration camps while boarding their horses in the most lavish and consecrated Jewish places of worship. The irony was lost on no one.

Situated near the synagogues were several tall pre-war brick buildings housing colorful eateries with names like Restauracja Zydowska, Rubinstein, and Ariel. Easily recognizable Jewish symbols adorned the signs on the cafes.

As I looked around, I felt the excitement start to build inside of me. "Jewish restaurants?" I blurted out enthusiastically, feeling like I had just run into an old friend in the most unlikely of places.

"Jewish style," Memel responded sheepishly.

Josh asked the question on everyone's minds. "What does that mean?"

Memel explained, "There are no Jews here anymore. These restaurants are owned and operated by Poles."

Mike needed to clarify. "You mean they're tourist traps?"

Our guide was silent.

My bubble burst.

"Poland's Jewish Epcot," I uttered sarcastically with a hint of regret. "Nothing here is authentic."

Memel bowed his head. "Not anymore."

In the center of the square, a Polish vendor had set up a kiosk. On his table, right next to the Pinocchio puppet and an assorted cast of character marionettes, were miniature wooden dolls carved and painted to resemble Orthodox rabbis, complete with long beards and prayer shawls. Each one had a zloty, the equivalent of a Polish penny, glued to the palm of its hand.

"What the hell are these!?" I demanded, wanting an explanation from the salesman. He seemed somewhat confused. It was obvious enough to him.

"*Zyd*," he answered flatly.

"I know it's a Jew! What is the meaning of *this*?" I pointed to the zloty.

"It's for good luck," Memel educated us quite innocently. "The Jew doll brings you wealth and financial success."

It felt like the oldest stereotype known to man had just me kicked in the stomach.

"I keep one in my kitchen," he added proudly. "On the shelf next to the macaroons."

# Chapter 33

$\mathcal{U}$pon entering the main square in Kazimierz, Sarah passed a convoy of Nazi trucks, tanks, and motorcycles. The loud, foreign rumblings were a sharp contrast to the neighborhood's typical quiet serenity. The ominous motorcade was headed toward the majestic Wawel Castle, which, in a matter of hours, would become the new headquarters for the SS in Krakow. There, in the throne room where Polish monarchs once held court, Nazi generals would delight in taking potshots with their rifles at the centuries-old hand-sculpted wooden faces of royalty staring down at them from the gloriously vaulted ceilings.

Sarah put her bags down in front of the cemetery and leaned for a moment on its wrought-iron fence.

Effie's bright green eyes peered out from the air holes in his carrying sack.

She inhaled. "Smells like Mama's kitchen," she said aloud. "So far, so good, Effie. It's not against the law to make *kugel*. Not yet, anyway."

Residents were trying to go about their business as usual. Some children played ball in the street.

Armed German officers surveyed the land, measured building circumferences, and made copious notes.

Sarah continued on her way. She passed a couple of Nazis painting a Star of David and the words "Jewish Owned" on the window of a kosher butcher shop. That seemed redundant, she thought.

She picked up the pace.

# Chapter 34

The remaining girls were quickly getting settled into Sosia's parents' house in Kazimierz. Those who had already unpacked were busy reading, studying, or chatting. Devorah softly strummed her guitar.

In the kitchen with Sosia's mother, Sarah sorted potatoes and sliced bread for the less fortunate.

"Thank you again for taking all of us in, Ruchul," Sarah said.

Ruchul smiled with both of her chins.

"Of course, what else would I do?"

Suddenly, there was an unexpected knock at the door. The girls froze. Ruchul started for the door. Sarah stopped her. "Allow me," Sarah insisted.

Sarah hurried through the parlor and slowly opened the door. Standing there was an old, destitute-looking woman.

"Are you here for food?" Sarah asked.

"No, I'm here for Hannah. Hannah Weiss," the woman answered wryly. "Is she here?"

Sarah was suspicious. "Who wants to know?"

Hannah, overhearing the conversation, raced to the door but cloaked herself behind Sarah.

"I'm an old friend of the family," the woman explained. "It's her Aunt Sophie," she continued. "She's taken ill. She needs her."

Out of concern, Hannah rushed to the forefront.

"Aunt Sophie?" she gasped. "I'll be right there."

Chaya bolted upstairs.

"Hannah..." Sarah was hesitant.

"It's okay, Mother Sarah," Hannah assured her. "I'll see her back to health and return as soon as I possibly can."

"But everything is so uncertain. What if we're no longer here, in this house? How will you—"

"Don't worry. Krakow is my city. I know it well. I will find you."

Chaya returned with Hannah's bag. "I gathered your things for you," Chaya said. "Since none of us have very much, it didn't take me long."

Hannah hugged her friend. "Thank you, Chaya. I'll come back soon." She flung her arms around Sarah and added, "God be with you. God be with all of you."

The girls watched as Hannah departed with the unlikely messenger.

Sarah waved good-bye. "God be with *you*, my little Hannahlah."

# Chapter 35

*R*egina and Manfred carried little Tania up a narrow flight of dimly lit stairs. Finally, they arrived at an unfamiliar apartment.

Angry voices of a man and a woman having a heated argument in German permeated the unmarked, gray metal door.

"Are you sure about this?" Manfred asked nervously.

"I'll never be sure about this," Regina answered in a hushed tone. "Our options are getting more limited every day. This is her best hope for survival. We have to put our trust in God and take this chance. For her sake. Let's get it done, as quickly as possible."

Manfred knocked softly on the door. The arguing inside the apartment came to an abrupt end.

"*Ja,*" responded a voice from the other side. It was so muted that neither Manfred nor Regina could discern if the voice belonged to the man or the woman.

Manfred looked at his wife hesitantly.

"Go ahead," she prompted him.

Manfred cleared his throat, then quietly began to recite a children's nursery rhyme.

*"Hupfen, hupfen, reiter..."*

Slowly, the door creaked open. An unusual-looking Aryan couple in their late thirties stood in the entryway of a modest flat.

The woman was tall, thin, and strikingly beautiful, with auburn red hair. Her husband, by contrast, was shorter and somewhat overweight, with a dark combover.

Tania, still in the safety of her mother's arms, looked perplexed.

"You will honor our agreement?" Regina asked anxiously.

"*Ja,*" replied the woman. "We will take good care of her while you are in hiding. No one will suspect that she is not our daughter." The woman smiled confidently as she ran her long, thin fingers through the child's coincidentally matching auburn curls.

Tania was getting agitated.

"And should we, please God, survive the war..." Manfred continued.

The man finished impatiently, "We shall give back the child upon your safe return."

"And if, God forbid, we don't make it..." Regina added.

The woman assured her, "She will have the best of everything we can offer her. And when she is old enough, we will tell her about you."

Regina mustered up every ounce of strength to fight back a tsunami of tears as she and Manfred kissed their daughter good-bye.

"*Mutti* loves you."

"*Vati* loves you too." Manfred choked.

They handed their child to the woman.

Frightened, Tania cried out and clung to her mother. She refused to be separated. The harder they tried to peel her out of Regina's arms, the louder she wailed.

Suddenly, a door downstairs opened and a strange voice called up the stairwell, "*Hallo!*"

Regina covered the baby's mouth.

There was silence for what felt like an eternity.

Finally, the downstairs apartment door closed.

"I am sorry," the man insisted. "This is too risky. We will be shot if we are caught hiding a Jewish child. You must go."

"Good luck to you," the woman said regretfully as she caressed Tania's unsettled cheek. "Good luck to *all* of you."

The husband reprimanded his wife, "I told you…" he began as he launched into a tirade and slammed the door shut.

# Chapter 36

*T*ania slept soundly on the soft rose-tinted crushed-velvet sofa. It had been a couple of days since the failed attempt to place her with a Christian couple. Plan B was in motion.

Manfred had a small bag packed. Regina handed him a copy of the family photo. She had tears in her eyes. "The extra copy," she prodded. "Keep it with you. Think of us often and pray that one day we will be reunited, as a family. That you and I may raise our daughter and grow old together, like we were meant to."

Manfred looked at the photo and smiled. He carefully placed it in the inside pocket of his long, tan overcoat.

"Regina, we will get through this, God willing. Concentrate on staying hidden with Tania. Frau Tietze will be here in an hour to get you to a safe house."

"You must tell me where you will be hiding," she demanded. "How will I know if you are okay? How will

I find you after the war?" I want to be able to check in with you. I'll *need* to hear your voice."

"If they think you know where I am, they'll torture you or worse..." Manfred beheld their daughter sleeping peacefully on a comfortable end of the couch. "They would harm our baby in an attempt to locate me. It's better you don't know. Somehow, someway, *I'll* come back to *you* after the war."

They embraced. Regina could no longer contain her sorrow. Her beautiful blue eyes flooded. Manfred pressed his lips against hers and wiped her tears.

He leaned over the sofa to kiss his slumbering daughter good-bye and stroked her baby-fine curls.

"God bless you and *Mutti, meine Tochter,*" he whispered like a guardian angel in her ear. "I'll always be with you. I'll always be with *both* of you."

Manfred turned back to Regina. He knew he had to remain strong for her. Now, more than ever, he needed to be her rock. "I love you, Regina. May God watch over you and our Faigele and keep you both safe and out of harm's way."

Regina was sobbing uncontrollably now. "Manfred, I love you too. Find us, Manfred, find us..."

Manfred held her one last time. He kissed her long and passionately. He picked up his bundle and headed for the door. With a tip of his favorite fedora, he added, "*Meine* Regina, only death could keep me from you and our precious little girl."

With that, he was gone.

Regina slumped to the floor.

Peeking out from under the sofa, she spotted one of Manfred's old hankies. It had scalloped edges and was embroidered with a lovely royal-blue M. She remembered this one. She had given it to him on their first wedding anniversary.

Tightening her grip on the hanky, her arm catapulted toward the door.

"Manfred!"

Wistfully, she retreated. It was too late. Manfred was gone.

Holding her husband's hanky close to her cheek, she inhaled the scent of it. Then, folding it neatly, she lovingly tucked it inside her loaded suitcase, which sat alongside the sofa where tiny Tania was still fast asleep.

# Chapter 37

$I$t was in the pre-dawn hours when Frau Tietze brought Regina and Tania into a meager one-room flat somewhere in Berlin. It had a bed, a bathroom, a sewing machine, and not much else.

"I'm sorry, Regina," Frau Tietze apologized. "This is the best I can do for now. The owner will stop by to bring you food. In exchange for your keep, you will sew for her husband's company. I told her you're an experienced seamstress."

"I see the machine," Regina acknowledged. "What type of sewing?"

"He provides services for the Reich," Tietze explained. "It's best not to ask too many questions. Do whatever she asks."

Frau Tietze placed a covered basket of supplies on the floor in front of the bed. "Here are some emergency necessities. I will bring more when I return."

"Frau Tietze, wait." Regina reached into her shoulder bag and produced an envelope. "These few photographs are the only memories I have left. Please keep them in a safe place for me until after the war." She placed the envelope in Tietze's right hand and secured it with her left.

Tietze checked the contents of the envelope. Gingerly sliding the cherished photographs out, she examined them, one by one.

There was a posed family portrait of Regina as a baby with her mother, father, four older sisters, and two older brothers. Regina, in a long white baby gown, was propped adorably on her mother's lap.

Regina and Manfred's regal-looking wedding portrait was next, then a picture of Tania with her doll, a copy of the Joel family photo, and finally, an old snapshot of Regina's sister Rosa with her young son, Josef.

Frau Tietze's face filled with sadness. She agreed to keep the photos.

Behind the photos, Tietze noticed some Deutschmarks.

"What is this?"

Regina winced. "I'm sorry it's not more."

Frau Tietze protested, "But I wasn't able to hide all three of you together. Maybe I could have—"

Regina insisted, "I can't thank you enough for all you've done for me and my family."

"I'm afraid I am no match for the Reich."

"Oh, but you are, Frau Tietze; you most certainly are."

Tietze feigned an uneasy smile.

Regina escorted Tietze to the door. The women embraced.

"When this is all over," Tietze wondered, "maybe you could tell them...in the midst of all the ugliness, there remained a few good Germans."

"Tell whom?" Regina asked curiously.

Frau Tietze choked back her tears. "Anyone who will listen."

# Chapter 38

*R*egina and Tania were sleeping cuddled together on the single bed. It had been about a week since Frau Tietze had brought them to the first of what would necessarily become several hiding places. The basket on the floor was practically empty. Mother and daughter were adjusting to longer periods of hunger between meager meals.

Suddenly, the owner of the flat charged in like the German tank she resembled. She dropped a pile of coats on the floor. The sound awakened Regina and Tania.

Regina was cautious but relieved to see another human being. "Oh, thank God. You must be—"

"Doesn't matter who I am," the woman retorted. "Did Tietze tell you that you must sew in exchange for your stay?"

Tania wiped the sleep from her eyes and reached for her doll.

"Yes," Regina answered.

"They all need repair. Get to work," the woman ordered. "I'll be back later to pick them up."

Regina got out of bed and picked up a coat. This one belonged to a child. "Pardon me," she inquired, "but whose coats are these?"

The woman grew impatient. "You can't pay because Jews have given all of their money and belongings to the Reich. We have a deal…you sew, you stay."

"Stolen," Regina clarified. "Surely, you must know that everything was stolen from us. Everything we worked so hard for our whole lives. We didn't *give* anything to the Reich."

The woman couldn't care less. She shrugged and headed for the door.

Regina panicked. "Wait!"

Now the woman was annoyed. "What?"

"Some food," Regina begged. "We finished everything Frau Tietze left us, and we are hungry. When you come back later, could you please bring some food for my baby and me?"

The woman smirked. "I will need something to trade." She cocked her square head in Tania's direction.

Tania held on to her doll closely, but it was the child's petite ruby earrings that had caught the woman's eye. They glimmered symmetrically on either side of the girl's disquieted face.

"Give me the earrings."

Regina objected, "But, they were my mother's, God rest her soul."

"You can't eat them," the woman quipped sarcastically.

Regina looked into her daughter's hungry, sallow eyes.

She relented.

Later that evening, Regina was busy laboring over the sewing machine.

There were two piles of coats on the floor. One pile was finished, and one still needed repairs.

Tania played with her doll on the bed.

The woman burst into the hiding place and deposited two hard, crusty pieces of bread and a thermos of watered-down brown liquid, something that resembled coffee but would taste more like mud, on the sewing table.

Regina could hardly believe her eyes. "That's it?" she asked in horrible disbelief. "We haven't eaten in days. That is all we get for my mother's ruby earrings?"

"It's the best I could do."

The woman quickly examined the two piles, callously scooped up the repaired coats, and stormed out.

Regina shared the stale bread with her daughter.

Tania watched as her mother irrepressibly choked on the combination of dry crumbs and drier tears.

# Chapter 39

*M*emel walked us up Miodowa Street into Zgoda Square next to the main railway station. It was mostly deserted except for several oddly oversized steel "chair" sculptures sporadically placed throughout the rather spacious open area.

"What is this place?" Mike asked.

Memel didn't usually take the time to think of a gentle way to describe things. At first, I held it against him. I thought he was rough and insensitive, but eventually, I let it go, chalking it up to his youth and inexperience.

"Where the Jews were forced to gather before boarding the trains to the camps," he answered matter of factly.

"What's with the chairs?" Josh asked politely.

"Another memorial?" I presupposed.

Memel nodded. *"Empty* chairs," he noted. "They represent the people who were murdered at the hands of the Nazi Fascists and are no longer here to sit in them."

Then he pointed to a tall, solid, arched concrete structure on the other side of the square. "Over there, one of the few remaining portions of the ghetto wall."

Following the direction of the pointed finger at the end of Memel's outstretched arm with great trepidation, we all exhaled at just about the same time.

"Not what I expected," Josh remarked.

"The sections were built to resemble giant headstones," I lectured, remembering some archived photos I had seen online.

Mike tugged on his collar. His breath got shallow. Josh noticed.

"Dad, you okay?"

Mike used his sleeve to wipe little beads of sweat that had formed on his otherwise strong forehead and responded in a troubling, unfamiliar staccato, "I— feel—claustrophobic. Can't—breathe."

The unimaginable was happening. Our rock was beginning to crumble.

"He needs to sit down," I said, trying to conceal my alarm.

Memel gazed around the desolate square. "Pick a chair," he said. "Any chair."

# Chapter 40

JUNE 1940

*Z*goda Square was teeming with people.

Sarah and the girls moved briskly through the desperate crowd. They tried to look inconspicuous despite the embarrassing white armbands with blue Stars of David shackled around their long cotton sleeves. Their small empty baskets floated back and forth in the early summer breeze. God willing, they would soon be weighted down with potatoes, turnips, or at least a shared loaf of bread. In a matter of mere months, the girls had gone from helping the needy to becoming the needy.

Horrible things were happening in the square. It had become a place of Jewish torture. Workers had begun construction of the headstone-shaped ghetto walls. Soon, the Jews would be caged in like animals.

Elderly pious rabbis, respected leaders of the community, were being forced to sweep the streets while Polish children pointed at them and laughed. Bearded Jewish men were being humiliated, their beards ripped off by sadistic Nazis' bare hands. Jewish community leaders were being rounded up and herded mercilessly into waiting cattle cars.

Sarah noticed a very long line of men and women, each of them carrying a single suitcase, being shuffled onto the trains. She was horrified to see that Yetta was among the doomed passengers in the queue. The two women exchanged a sorrowful glance. It was obvious to Sarah that Yetta was broken. Tears trailed down the headmistress's bony cheeks. Even the tight creases in her brow had surrendered. She inched forward.

Sarah mouthed, "God be with you" and pointed the girls in the opposite direction so that they would not have to witness the deportation of their former headmistress. Chaya started to follow her teacher's gaze, but Sarah quickly turned her around and marched her up toward the others. Looking back one final time, Sarah saw Yetta wave as she boarded the ill-fated train. She bottled her emotions and kept the girls moving.

Walking closely together past the Nazis, Sarah and the girls camouflaged a cauldron of soup inside their tightly knit circle.

En route to their destination, they were unexpectedly derailed by the construction crews.

"We'll have to go another way," instructed Sarah. She thought for a moment. "Devorah, you and the girls slip down Miodowa. Chaya, Frida, Sosia, Pesia, and I will create a diversion. Meet us back in the square when you are done."

Devorah and her troop did as they were told and secretly began to pass the soup cauldron down Miodowa Street.

Sarah approached an apple cart. She appealed to the poor vendor, "Please forgive me."

She kicked the stand out from under the cart, spilling hand-polished red apples onto the street. A crowd of starving people descended upon the scattered fruit. The Nazis were distracted by the commotion and immediately tended to the crowd to restore order.

Sarah, Chaya, Frida, Sosia, and Pesia dashed off, past sacred Torah scrolls and other precious loot stolen from smoldering synagogues, piled high and engulfed in flames.

Sarah and the girls watched helplessly as innocent children from the orphanage were paraded in their Sabbath best toward the trains.

One terrified orphan wandered out of formation and hid behind Sarah's skirt. Sarah instinctively covered the orphan in the folds of the material, and the girls gathered to conceal her.

Staying one step ahead of the Nazis, they sneaked to an unfinished section of the wall.

Through the opening, they saw a pair of shiny black boots march by.

Sarah waited, then peeked through. "Now," she ordered.

Chaya, Frida, and the tiny, scrappy stowaway squeezed through to the Aryan side.

Sarah called instructions through the opening. "Just what you can carry. Take her to the monastery. They will place her. Go!"

The girls and the orphan disappeared on the other side of the wall.

Meanwhile, Devorah and crew were successfully making their way down Miodowa Street.

Patrolling Nazis approached, and the girls dodged them by scooting down a nearby alley. They watched from the safety of an alcove as the Nazis passed, then they returned to the ghetto street, carrying the heavy cauldron from person to person, feeding soup to the starving families on Midowa.

Devorah kept a watchful eye.

Back at the unfinished wall, Sarah, Sosia, and Pesia hovered in front of the hole that the others had climbed through. They tried to avoid eye contact and to look as inconspicuous as possible.

One fresh-faced Nazi passing by looked suspiciously at them and nearly stopped, but before he could question them, he was called onward by his commanding officer.

On the Aryan side of the wall, Chaya and Frida successfully delivered the orphan to the monastery.

Nuns took the child and in exchange offered a sack of potatoes to the girls. No questions were asked.

"Thank you," the girls said as they juggled the cumbersome sack between them and made a quick getaway.

A short time later, missions completed, Sarah's group safely reunited with Devorah's group in the square as planned. The soup cauldron now contained the sack of potatoes. The girls closed ranks in order to keep it out of sight.

Seemingly unaware of the inhumanity going on around him, a highly decorated Nazi played lovingly with his dog. Krakow District's SS and police chief, Kommandant Julian Schoerner, in his late forties, hard looking with sharp features, was full of joy as he fed his huge, ominous-looking German shepherd a handful of treats from one of the pockets of his crisp brown uniform. He patted the dog on the head and scratched him playfully behind the ear. A cigar dangled from the corner of Schoerner's crooked mouth.

Sarah noticed the affection between the man and his dog. "Could it be?" she wondered. He was one of *them,* and yet, there with his beloved pet, amidst all of this inhumanity, he seemed almost human.

A much younger officer, certainly one of lesser rank, Claude Bauer, pushing thirty, with wavy ash-blond hair and piercing aqua eyes, stood behind Schoerner, savoring his senior officer's moment.

Suddenly, an enthusiastic Jewish toddler approached the dog and stroked his thick brownish black fur. The boy's young mother ran after to stop him. "Teodor, no!" she pleaded, her skinny frame nearly convulsing in desperation.

Schoerner became enraged. "You touched my dog, you filthy little Jew?!"

Schoerner gave the signal to his henchman. Without a second thought, Bauer shot the child point blank in the head.

The boy's mother screamed out. Bauer took careful aim precisely at her head too. Another shot rang out. Both mother and child lay dead in the street.

Horrified, the girls shrieked. Sarah signaled them to take flight, but it was too late. Bauer had spotted them.

"*Halten!*" he ordered.

Bauer, Schoerner, and the dog, on a thick chained leash, approached. The Nazis were smiling. It was time for a little fun, and Sarah knew it.

"So, what do we have here?" Bauer queried cheerfully. "A mother out for a stroll with her lovely daughters?"

Schoerner enjoyed a long, exaggerated puff of his cigar. He sized them up. "*Nein,*" he said. "I think we have a dedicated teacher and her devoted students, *ja?*"

He leered. There was something about Sarah that he found attractive. The girls squirmed.

Sarah stood her ground. She remained unemotional.

"*Ja, ja.* Jews love their books," Schoerner continued.

He gleefully motioned over his shoulder at the burning pile of Torah scrolls in the square as if he needed to prove his point. "You know, teacher, I have many enlisted men who love to 'read.'" His use of allegory was repugnant.

Sarah tucked the girls behind her skirt.

Schoerner remained unsettlingly calm.

"Where do these lessons take place? Where can my men find such lovely books that they might devour each and every page?"

Sarah said nothing. He must fancy himself as clever, she thought. She could barely tolerate his disgusting metaphors.

Schoerner was practically salivating as he looked over the girls like the cat that was anxious to swallow the canary.

The girls began to whimper.

Schoerner insisted, "I asked you, *Fraulein,* what is the exact location of your place of learning?" His voice was getting louder, his tone more forceful. "Jewish schools were ordered to close, but it looks like your class is still in session." He inhaled from his cigar and examined it.

Sarah's face remained unchanged. From across the square, both Nazis and their victims were beginning to take notice. A small crowd of onlookers formed.

In the crowd was a familiar-looking young man.

Mordechai wore a cap. Most of his face was concealed by a lightweight, olive-green scarf—except for his chocolate brown eyes which grew angrier by the minute.

Schoerner slowly exhaled a cloud of smoke. He nodded to Bauer, who pulled out his gun and placed it squarely on Sarah's temple.

"I will ask you one last time, you stupid Jew," Schoerner said firmly. "Where is the school?"

The girls were now crying and shaking. A couple of them prayed under their breath.

Bauer cocked his weapon.

Sarah broke her silence. "Wait!"

Schoerner smirked, believing he had won.

Sarah spoke to her girls. "Daughters of Abraham, Isaac, and Jacob, my precious girls, turn away and do not witness the evil of mankind."

The girls, now moaning and sobbing, followed Sarah's orders, as always. In the confusion, a couple of them began to lose their grip and almost dropped the hidden cauldron, but Devorah and Frida steadied it and managed to keep it concealed.

The crowd watched in agony. No one dared to inter-
fere. Even Mordechai, noticing how heavily armed the
Nazis were, nervously paced, at a loss for what to do.
Schoerner's dog kept him and the others at bay.

Schoerner was infuriated. "*Jude!* Even with a gun to
your Jewish head, you refuse to answer."

He waved off Bauer, who put his gun back in its holster. It wasn't time, Schoerner decided. Still, he
needed to punish her—publicly.

Schoerner grabbed Sarah's left hand and turned it
palm side up. The scornful expression on his despica-
ble face turned to pleasure as he proceeded to burn
her with his lit cigar. Sarah's skin sizzled until the cigar
extinguished.

Schoerner flicked what was left of the cigar to the
ground.

A couple of the girls watched fearfully over their
shoulders with one eye. They screamed and cried out
a mixture of both terror and relief.

Schoerner's German shepherd barked loudly.

Sarah held in her pain. In spite of her torture, she
needed to remain brave for the sake of her girls.

"Beautiful hands are wasted on Jewish swine," he
declared. "Now, what shall we do with that Jewish
face?"

Schoerner pulled another cigar from his pocket, situated it crudely in his mouth, and struck a match.

Chaya couldn't bear to see her beloved teacher suf-
fer more. She had to think fast.

"Stanislava 10!" she blurted out.

Schoerner was pleased. "That's a good little Jew."

He reached into another pocket, pulled out a candy, and tossed it at Chaya, who had begun crying so hard, she was hyperventilating.

Schoerner returned his focus to Sarah. "Until we meet again."

His gloved hand reached for her charred flesh. He squeezed it tightly, then dropped it. It fell like a raw potato.

Sarah felt overwhelmingly woozy, and she began to faint. Mordechai rushed over to help the girls catch her.

Laughing victoriously, Schoerner, with his dog and henchman, moved on to look for their next source of amusement.

Mordechai and the girls supported Sarah out of Zgoda Square. As they departed, Chaya tossed the repulsive piece of candy to the ground.

A swarm of starving bystanders swooped down like vultures to retrieve it.

# Chapter 41

*B*ack at Sosia's house, Sarah lay, nearly passed out, on the double bed in Sosia's parents' room. A faded floral duvet covered her, and a fluffy white pillow separated her tired head from an arched European walnut headboard.

Effie jumped up and planted himself next to her.

Mordechai diligently tore off his armband and wrapped it around her burnt hand.

"I won't be needing this anymore," he said mostly to himself.

Although feeling extremely weak, Sarah managed a sincere expression of gratitude. "Thank you, Mordechai."

Effie settled in, curling his tail around his body and tucking it under his chin. He closed his eyes and began to snore, a subtle, wheezy cat snore. The sound comforted Sarah.

"Sarah," Mordechai said. His voice was initially calm and soothing. "It's getting worse. I don't know if you heard..."

He navigated the difficulty of what he was about to say. "There was a massacre in Mielec."

Sarah shook her head. Her eyes widened.

Mordechai's voice took on a sense of urgency as he recounted the horrific event.

"The Nazis waited for Rosh Hashanah. They rounded up all of the Jews and locked them in the synagogue. Then they set the building on fire. All of them, packed inside, innocent men, women, and children. Burned alive. Those who couldn't fit inside were lined up along the perimeter of the synagogue's outside walls and shot to death."

Tears streamed down Sarah's distressed face.

"We've had enough," Mordechai declared. "We're organizing. My friends Shimshon and Dolek and I, along with some others, are smuggling necessities. Our comrades Eduard and Yitzchak have contacts in Warsaw. We are gathering weapons. Soon we will begin sabotaging German installations."

They embraced. He felt he needed to tell her more. "Do you know '*Apteka Pod Orlem,*' 'Under the Eagle?'" he asked.

Sarah summoned the strength to speak. "The only non-Jewish-owned pharmacy on Zgody Square?" she responded. "It's being barricaded inside the new ghetto walls."

"Yes. That's the one. Tadeusz Pankiewicz, the pharmacist, is risking his life to help us. He is providing medicines for the infirm at no charge. He is offering hair dye so some can make a disguise to elude the Nazis, and tranquilizers to quiet children hidden during raids by the Gestapo. We are working underground at the pharmacy. With Tadeusz's help, we can get food and information. His staff helps us hide those that must be hidden. He is truly righteous among the nations."

She interrupted him, "Mordechai, do you remember the day we met?"

"How could I forget?"

"You said if there is anything anyone has that someone else needs, you are the man to deliver it." She pressed, "Remember?"

"Yes, I remember. Of course, I said that before the Germans marched into Poland," he explained.

"If there is something I need, could I count on you to get it?" she beseeched him.

"For you, Sarah, I'd die trying."

Mordechai took Sarah's good hand in his and looked sweetly into her midnight-blue eyes. "Tell me, Sarah, what is it that you need?"

# Chapter 42

*R*egina could see the sun setting from a small tear in the dirty old shade that covered the window of their hiding place in the secret apartment.

She reached into Frau Tietze's basket and pulled out two thick, white candles and a half-used book of matches. She placed the candles securely on the sewing table.

"Come, Tania," she called to her daughter. "It's time to welcome the Sabbath."

Regina retrieved Manfred's handkerchief from her purse and placed it gently over her head. Tania approached the table, habitually excited. She reveled in the weekly Sabbath rituals. She watched intently as Regina lit the candles. The flames reflected in her brightening blue eyes. She imitated her mother as Regina waved her hands over the candles three times, then covered her eyes before reciting the traditional Hebrew prayer. "*Baruch Atah Ashem, Elokeynu Melech Haolam. Asher Kidishanu.* Blessed are You, Lord, our

God, King of the Universe, Who has sanctified us with His commandments..."

Inside Sosia's house in Krakow, Sarah and the girls were performing the same religious ritual.

"*B'Mitzvothav Vitzivanu Lihadlik Ner Shel Shabbos.* And commanded us to light the Sabbath candles." Sarah removed her hands from her eyes and the lace covering from her head.

It was the perfect time for a mini-lesson, she thought. "The great Zionist thinker Ahad Ha-am wrote, 'More than the Jewish people have kept the Sabbath, the Sabbath has kept the Jewish people.'"

She and the girls were hopeful as they exchanged greetings.

"Good Shabbos."

It wasn't long before a giant wave of peace seemed to ebb through the small dwelling.

Chaya stared sadly at her teacher.

Always intuitive of her students' emotions, Sarah asked, "What is it, Chayalah?"

"Mother Sarah," Chaya began solemnly, "do you think we will ever see our families again?"

The room got quiet. All of the girls anxiously awaited Sarah's reply.

Sarah measured her words. "If it is God's will," she assured them.

Sarah put her loving arms around Chaya and the girls standing nearest her. "For now, *this* is our family."

# Chapter 43

egina's hands worked tirelessly on an old Singer sewer, circa 1910. Her fingers ran the black thread through the bobbin, up past the gold ornamentation on the shoulder of the machine, and back down through the sharp, pointy needle. Her foot pressed rhythmically on the treadle.

Wearing no makeup, her reading glasses balanced at the tip of her nose, her brown hair tucked completely inside a colorless knit scarf, she cut, sewed, and methodically threw scraps of fabric into a nearby wastebasket.

On the bed, toddler Tania happily prattled on with her doll.

A loud banging at the front door shook both mother and daughter to the core.

Regina removed her glasses and motioned to her daughter to hide under the bed.

With Tania safely out of view, Regina cautiously answered the door.

Standing at the doorway were two Gestapo officers. They held a photo.

The first officer spoke. "Regina Joel?" he demanded.

Regina swallowed her fear. Instinctively, she played dumb. "Who?"

The second officer showed her the picture. It was her on a better, healthier day, with full, dark, wavy hair, mascara, lipstick, and glasses.

"We are looking for Regina Joel," he repeated.

Regina stayed cool. "*Nein.* Don't know her."

"She is traveling with a little girl."

"*Keine kinder hier.* No children here."

She peered backward for a moment and noticed Tania's doll sprawled, face up on the floor. Turning back, she desperately tried to hide her alarm.

The first officer strained to look past her into the apartment.

Thinking quickly, she unfastened the top button of her unseasonably heavy dress. Not knowing how long they'd be on the run, she had mostly packed for colder weather.

Delicately, she fanned herself. "Very warm in Berlin today. Will there be anything else, gentlemen?"

The Nazis were easily distracted. While they stared at her cleavage, she glanced backward once again to see Tania's little arm retrieve the doll and pull it out of sight.

The SS men, however, were only temporarily amused.

Without warning, the first officer rammed the door open, and from the doorstep, the two men scanned the apartment. Regina held her breath.

"If you see this woman and her daughter, you are ordered to denounce them to the SS," concluded the second officer. "We pay stipends for each Jew turned in." He gave her the once-over. "Looks like you, *Fraulein*, could use the money."

Regina wanted to spit. Instead, she nodded.

The two officers gave Regina the now all too familiar salute. "*Heil Hitler!*"

Regina closed the door and locked it.

"Ok, little bird," she whispered, "time to fly."

# Chapter 44

#10 STANISLAVA STREET

10:00 PM

*T*here was a chill in the night air as the tormen-
tors from Zgoda Square, Schoerner and Bauer,
with several other armed Nazis, raced up the stairs of
the vacant Beth Jacob School building.

Carelessly, they kicked over furniture, smashed in
doors, stomped on leftover belongings, broke mirrors,
and destroyed everything in sight.

They searched every empty room.

Realizing they had been duped, Schoerner flew into
an uncontainable rage. "Find them!" he bellowed.

# Chapter 45

*I*t was in the early hours of the morning when Frau Tietze used a key to let herself into the hidden apartment. She carried a small basket of food and supplies.

"*Hallo?*" she called with some trepidation.

She was greeted with silence. The place was barren.

She searched the flat for any remnants of her dear friends. Her only findings were Regina's reading glasses and an empty bottle of peroxide in the wastebasket.

Tietze felt the breath leave her body. She fell to her knees and made the sign of the cross. "In the name of the Father, the Son, and the Holy Spirit..."

# Chapter 46

*N*ight fell over Kazimierz, and in the dark basement of Sosia's house, the girls sat on benches around a long rectangular table.

Candles illuminated the room.

Each maiden scribbled something on a torn piece of paper. The girls were visibly shaken.

Sarah stared sadly into the flickering candlelight as she stroked Effie with her scarred, trembling hand.

Outside, Hannah attempted to return to her schoolmates. She looked around to make sure she wasn't noticed as she approached Sosia's house.

Spotting Nazi officers milling around the front of the place, she silently sneaked around to the back, to an unguarded window, and peeked in.

Hannah was not surprised by what she witnessed. She was all too familiar with this ritual. They had done it dozens of times before, when something important needed to be agreed upon. Sarah had instituted the policy. Every girl's voice would be heard. They were voting. But what? What were they deciding?

Chaya collected the votes in the apron of her skirt. She dumped them on the table in front of Sarah. Sarah looked over each one carefully.

Unwavering, she announced, "It's unanimous."

Effie leaped off her lap.

The realization hit Hannah like incoming Luftwaffe. She burst into tears and pounded her hands on the thick glass.

"No!" she cried out.

The noise alerted a nearby patrolling Nazi, and Hannah was hastily run off by the sounds of approaching doom.

# Chapter 47

*M*ike was still a bit queasy following his full-fledged panic attack.  He straggled some-what behind as Memel led us past the haunting, larger-than-life chair sculptures to an unassuming two-story building in the northwest corner of the square.

The lower level stood out with a fresh coat of white paint.  Parallel to the intersection was a pair of long, thin, barn-red doors.  Each door comprised eight rectangular panels, each panel thickly trimmed in black. A sign over the double doors read, "Apteka Pod Orlem."

In front of the building, a newish silver bicycle was tethered to a street sign, and two Polish boys played some type of marble game close to the curb.

Memel strutted past the boys, skipped up the curb, landed in front of the big red doors, and beamed. "This is the Under the Eagle Pharmacy."

Mike timidly checked out the surroundings.

Josh peered curiously over the shoulders of the Polish boys to gain a better understanding of their game.

From the street, my eyes took in all of the architecture.

On the upper level, where the gray façade peeled back to reveal faded ruddy brick, there was a small balcony.

Two long windows draped in sheer white linens were propped open. The curtains blew gently in the breeze.

On the railing of the balcony hung a box dotted with tiny, unidentifiable crimson flowers. On the balcony itself grew lots and lots of lush green plants.

"Does it still function as a drugstore?" I wanted to know.

Memel was quick to answer. "Now, it's a museum," he proudly pointed out. "Would you like to go—"

Before he could finish his sentence, I was through the doors.

Standing in the small foyer of what had once been the legendary pharmacy's entrance, my eyes grew wide.

With my family still on the other side, the heavy museum doors swung and shut tightly behind me.

A bell rang.

# Chapter 48

*A* bell rang. The heavy pharmacy doors swung closed.

Sarah entered the busy shop and took her place in line behind a few Polish customers.

Working the counter, the pharmacist, Tadeusz Pankiewicz, was an unassuming-looking man. He wore a long white lab coat with a crisp, black bow tie protruding from the collar. His black hair was meticulously combed back, and his eyes were tepid and full of compassion.

Tadeusz's young, attractive employees, Irena, Helena, and Aurelia filled orders. The line moved quickly.

Sarah approached the counter.

"May I help you?" Pankiewicz inquired politely.

"I, uh, have this prescription to be filled," Sarah announced, her voice shaking. She handed him a note.

He read it carefully, glanced from side to side, then responded calmly, "I do not carry this in stock." Nonchalantly, he called to his first assistant. "Irena, please take this woman's information so that we may contact her when her special order comes in."

Sarah knew the protocol. She had been coached. "God bless you," she replied.

Irena, a creamy-complected beauty with a dark brown bob, stopped what she was doing and sprung into action. She escorted Sarah past a row of wooden stools to the pharmacist's private office in the back of the store, then quickly closed the door behind them and locked it. "Help me," she instructed Sarah.

Together, they moved a tall bookcase to reveal a hidden door, which Irena pried open halfway. Gently, she shoved Sarah inside.

Irena closed the door immediately, leaving Sarah in the dark. Sarah heard Irena struggle to push the bookcase back into position. She pressed her face against the back of the closed door and whispered anxiously, "Thank you."

It was a moment before Sarah realized that she was teetering on the top step of a long, narrow staircase.

Carefully, she used an unstable wooden railing to guide her down into the cavernous blackness.

At the bottom of the stairs, she heard distant voices. One of them sounded familiar. She followed the gradually increasing volume past a series of dark storage rooms to another closed door. Summoning her courage, she slowly pushed the door open. "Mordechai?"

The small room was brightly lit.

Sarah's eyes took a second to make the adjustment.

There were young men and women organizing food, medicines, and information.

Dolek, Shimshon, Yitzchak, and Eduard, four young, good-looking fellows, were seated at the table closest to the door. The table was covered with glass bottles, wires, and containers of petrol.

Dolek, thin and clean-shaven, with an infectious smile, spotted Sarah. He jumped up to meet her but stopped short of extending his hand, respecting her Orthodox upbringing.

"You must be Sarah," he said with a big, toothy grin. "Beautiful school teacher, just as Mordechai described. Nice to meet you. I am Dolek."

Sarah felt the tension in her body release. "Ah, Dolek. Mordechai has also told me much about you. Is it true that your real name is Adolph, or was Mordechai joking?"

Dolek laughed heartily. "Yes, it's true, and how very unfortunate for me. But how were Mother and Father to know? Please, don't hold it against me."

"Don't worry," she assured him.

Dolek made the necessary introductions.

"This is Shimshon and Yitzchak."

The boys respectfully responded, "Hello."

Not to be ignored, Eduard cleared his throat.

"Oh, excuse me," Dolek added. "And *this* is Eduard."

"Mo told us many nice things about you," Eduard, dark and dashing, revealed. "Nice to finally make your acquaintance."

"Mo?" Sarah wondered aloud.

"Moses!" Eduard clarified. "That's what I call Mordechai because he will lead us out of this Egypt. He will deliver us from this hell."

Dolek decided to rescue Sarah. "Mordechai!"

Motioning to the far side of the protracted room, he informed her, "He's over there, Sarah, with my wife, Minka, and Shimshon's Justyna."

Mordechai, who had been busy working on the underground newspaper with the dark-haired and beautiful but tough Zionist brides, rushed toward Sarah. He was happy to see her, yet deeply concerned.

"Sarah! Does this mean..."

"It's been decided." As hard as it was for her to say, it was even more difficult to see him take the news. "And we've been relocated inside the ghetto."

"I heard. I'm sorry." He took her hand in his. "Sarah, I'll need some time to organize what you're asking for. We are moving our headquarters to the Aryan side. We'll have better access to supplies there. Besides, it's getting too risky, and we don't want to put Tadeusz in jeopardy. He's already done so much for us. As soon as I can, I will find a way to get it to you."

"Please hurry, Mordechai. They've been taunting us. I must protect my girls."

Mordechai grabbed Sarah and looked directly into her sad eyes.

She glanced at his strong hands holding firmly onto her burdened shoulders. She knew that an Orthodox Jewish woman should not be touched by any man who was not her husband. All things considered, she didn't really care.

"Sarah, are you sure?"

She felt as if she were melting. "As sure as I am about my faith in God and my feelings for you, Mordechai."

There, she said it. Mordechai managed a bittersweet smile, which quickly faded.

Sarah continued, "For me, there is no other choice..." She got lost in his gaze for a moment, then finally explained, "This is why I'm here." She realized the truth of her words the moment they left her lips.

Soon, she noticed that the resistance fighters were humming their fight song.

Their voices rose to a crescendo.

She listened tearfully to their battle cry.

"From land all green with palms, to land all white with snow, we now arrive with all our pain and woe. Where our blood sprayed out and came to touch the land, there our courage and our faith will rise and stand."

The partisans assembled homemade Molotov cocktails as they continued their chant.

Mordechai joined in. Sarah closed her eyes and let the words roll around her head and permeate her consciousness.

"This song was written with our blood and not with lead. It's not a song of the little birds out in the free. It was our people, among the toppling barricades, that sang this song and fought courageous till the end."

To Sarah, "The Song of the Partisans" resonated like a march and comforted like an anthem, but in her heart, she knew exactly what it was.

It was a promise.

# Chapter 49

*T*he late-afternoon sun was giving way to dusk over a sprawling fruit farm on the outskirts of Berlin.

A newly dyed platinum-blond Regina and her little Tania were escorted past a grove of peach trees to a sturdy wooden toolshed behind the main farmhouse by a stocky farm frau.

Tania carried her doll by one arm.

"You can eat whatever you find on the ground," allowed the farm frau.

Regina and Tania instinctively gathered a few peaches from the ground and stuffed their pockets.

"*Vielen Dank*, thank you very much," Regina said gratefully.

They passed between rows of caged rabbits. Tania couldn't resist. She stopped to admire the adorable furry animals. She put her finger into one of the cages to pet a receptive bunny on its twitching pink nose.

"We raise them here," the farm frau explained.

"Can I hold one?" Tania asked innocently.

Regina jumped in. "Oh, *Liebchen*, I don't think so..."

The woman looked around. It was quiet.

"Well, I suppose it would be okay," she acknowledged. "But briefly. I've got to get you two into the shed before anyone sees."

The woman swung the door open and took out a very large, long-haired albino bunny with big floppy ears.

Tania handed her doll to Regina.

The farm frau carefully placed the rabbit in Tania's tiny arms. The small girl could barely get a grip on the huge creature.

Regina smiled approvingly. She allowed Tania to cuddle the rabbit for a few short minutes.

Regina's anxiety was building as she slipped a few coins to the farm frau. "For your trouble," she whispered.

The farm frau remained expressionless as she accepted the transaction. It was just business, after all.

"Okay, Tania," Regina interjected. "Let's put her back in her cage now so we can get into our hiding place."

Tania looked into the rabbit's large red oval eyes as she spoke to her newfound friend. "You are not free either."

# Chapter 50

*A* self-imposed hush veiled the neighborhood surrounding an old rundown apartment house in a poor section of Berlin on this particular evening. A convoy of Nazi police cars pulled up hastily in front of the dark, silent building.

Nazis and their vicious dogs flooded the unassuming entrance and started up the central staircase. They reached the decaying third floor and rounded the moldy hallway corner. A single lightbulb flickered from the cobweb-covered glass fixture in the ceiling.

An old man in a white undershirt and pants held up by thin, charcoal gray suspenders emerged from his apartment. He pointed to the next door down. "*Jude,*" he said, barely moving his thin, slick lips.

The Nazis positioned themselves in front of the indicated door. The dogs barked.

"*Juden, Raus,* Jews, out!" they demanded.

The old man stood motionless and watched as the Nazis kicked down the door and forced their way into the still apartment.

Screams and shrieks permeated the hallway. Nazis shouted orders. A few shots were fired. Things crashed; property was destroyed.

Moments later, the Nazis reemerged with Manfred, their rifles in his back. He was well dressed in a shirt and tie under his smart-looking long tan overcoat. He situated his signature hat squarely on his head. He looked very dignified.

The Nazis ordered him out of the building.

Manfred noticed his informer still in the filthy hallway and eyeballed him. "Looks like I've been fixing the wrong leak," Manfred murmured.

The man retreated into his apartment. Manfred heard him secure the lock on his neglected door. Peeling paint chips floated insipidly to the concrete floor.

The impatient Nazis pushed Manfred onward, down the dusty, dimly lit staircase. The paint chips cracked and crumbled under the weight of his well-worn shoes.

Once outside, the Nazis ordered Manfred onto a waiting truck. He had no choice but to comply.

On the truck, Manfred found a number of other recently captured Jews, including an attractive woman with blond shoulder-length hair with her two children: a fussy baby boy and a shy young girl. The girl was about the same age as his Tania would be now, he figured.

God, how he missed her.

The woman made eye contact with Manfred. "A couple of months ago, Goebbels proclaimed Berlin *Judenfrei*," she said. "Do you think he finally got his wish? Are we the last Jews in Berlin?"

"I hope not," he answered.

"How many could possibly be left?" she asked urgently.

"At least two..." He rubbed his cold hands together as his determined eyes misted up. "...I pray."

Regina and Tania snuggled in front of a small fire behind the toolshed. Tania warmed her frigid hands. Regina cracked a twig, keeping an ever-vigilant eye on the surrounding woods. Suddenly, she was overcome with an inexplicable, undeniably sick feeling in her heart.

"*Mutti,* what is it?"

Snapping out of her temporary trance, Regina gained clarity and pushed her premonition aside. She tossed another broken twig into the fire. "It's okay, *Liebchen.*"

With the back of her hand, she caressed her baby's precious face.

For now, Regina had managed to pacify her daughter. But she couldn't convince herself. Something was terribly wrong. She could feel it. She pulled Tania closer and tried to warm her daughter's dainty shoulders.

Together, they stared into the rising flames, watching the billowy smoke ascend toward the heavens.

# Chapter 51

JANUARY 20, 1944

Smokestacks at Auschwitz-Birkenau were erupt-
ing like volcanoes, magnetically charging the
frosty atmosphere.

The train whistled as it came to a complete stop on
the *Judenramp* outside the colossal extermination
camp.

The doors to the cattle car made an unsettling noise
as they slid wide open.

Flashlights streamed into the dark, frozen wooden
boxcar, shedding light on Manfred and 47 other Jewish
men, women, and children, including the young
mother, her baby, and little girl from the roundup.

Guard dogs barked loudly.

Shivering from the cold, Manfred and the others
rose from the floor, squinting from the blinding Nazi
flashlights. Disoriented from the trip and unable to
recognize his surroundings, Manfred gained focus and

noticed outside, a layer of snow on the ground. He could see his own breath in the bone-chilling night air.

"*Achtung, Juden!*" shouted one Nazi. "Get onto the trucks. We will collect your personal belongings and return them to you after your shower and disinfectant."

Manfred was shoved off the train and hit the icy earth hard. He steadied himself. The air was unforgivingly bitter, and the wind challenged his gait.

# Chapter 52

*M*emel pulled his van up to a lone boxcar on the train tracks. No one moved.

We had just come from a Sabbath morning service at the centuries-old Remu Synagogue in Kazimierz. After being greeted by the gregarious, middle-aged gentleman who managed the building, the son of a Jew who had survived because his name was included on Schindler's list, I selected a seat in the elevated women's section separated by a white polka-dotted sheer curtain at the back of the surprisingly small sanctuary. Surrounded by a virtual UN of other women, mostly tourists like me who were speaking a variety of different tongues, I realized that although we couldn't understand each other, we were united by one thing...the Hebrew in the prayer books. Looking around, I noticed that, despite our geographical differences, we were all on the same page. Literally.

In the meantime, front and center, Mike and Josh received a hearty welcome by the larger-than-life rabbi.

"Jews?" the rabbi optimistically asked my husband.

"Yes," Mike confirmed.

The rabbi threw his prayer shawl-covered arms around my boys and escorted them to two of the best straight-backed, hard wooden bench seats in the house, right next to the decoratively scrolled, iron gate-enclosed Holy Ark.

Fearing that we were trying to "squeeze too much in"—or maybe they just wanted to sleep a little later—Mike and Josh had been reluctant to attend services that morning, but I insisted. Pleading my case, I explained that worship would be just the Vitamin B shot we would need to get us through this highly anticipated and most dreaded day of our entire trip, the day we would visit Auschwitz-Birkenau.

Turned out, I was right.

And so one Mourner's Kaddish and an *Adon Olam* later, we arrived in an area just outside the most heinous place on earth.

After a few extracted moments, we climbed uneasily out of Memel's van. Our nerves were already fraying. Out of respect for the dead, I wore the modest black gauze skirt I had packed and an army-green knit top due largely to a misguided sense that at some point I might feel the need to fight or, at the very least, flee. Blame it on a historic compulsion for self preservation. Mike and Josh did their level best to kick it up a notch with khakis and muted pastel-colored polo shirts.

Within seconds, a small, dark-blue vehicle arrived at the site as well. The driver of the car got out and approached us purposefully. In his early thirties, clean-shaven and with brown wavy hair, he had movie-star looks. His demeanor was very low key. We would soon come to recognize him as the knowledge-able, patient, and sympathetic person that he was. And we would learn what made him that way.

Memel greeted the mystery man with a handshake and a bear hug. They seemed to be old friends.

Our guide made the introductions. "This is Wiktor," Memel said. "He will escort you through the camp. His father, a non-Jewish survivor of Auschwitz-Birke-nau, is the museum's curator."

We were impressed on so many levels.

Wiktor greeted each one of us with a warm, friendly handshake. For some reason, he had an immediate calming effect on me. I decided to let Mike and Josh know. They always trusted my instincts.

"We're in good hands here," I told them.

Memel nodded in agreement.

Wiktor smiled and went right to work. "We are standing on the *Judenramp*," he explained. "Before the Nazis extended the tracks into Birkenau, the trains stopped here."

I approached the old boxcar for a closer look. Mike and Josh sensed that they should maintain a respectful distance. And so they did. I cursed the tracks, the iron rails to purgatory placed there by Satan himself. I kicked them with the heels of my sandals' soft soles. *How ineffective,* I thought. Why? Why didn't the Allies destroy them when they had the chance? I struggled.

Wiktor continued, "Jews and other prisoners were transferred to trucks and driven the remaining 800 meters into the camp."

Manfred turned to help the children and the elders unload from the boxcar. A Nazi guard ordered him onto the truck.

"*Schnell,* quickly!" he hollered.

As soon as all of the innocents were loaded onto the waiting trucks, a harsh-looking female Nazi approached with a basket.

While the guard collected valuables from the others, Manfred swiftly pulled off his gold wedding ring and slipped it in his mouth, underneath his tongue.

The group was then driven through the main gate at Birkenau and unloaded onto the selection ramp.

The trucks containing the prisoners' belongings continued the drive east, past endless rows of barracks, through the massive camp, to the warehouse known as Canada, where the loot would be sorted by female prisoners.

The Jews were instructed to walk straight down the path another 800 meters to the 'Showers.'

A group of Nazi guards looked over the new arrivals as they filed past.

One noticed strong, fit, 33-year-old Manfred. "That one could work," he commented.

Another Nazi official, holding a clipboard, responded, "There will be no selections tonight. Orders from the *Reichsfuehrer.* We have plenty of workers. Besides," he half-joked, "the Russians are getting closer, and we have been instructed to 'speed up production.'"

The guards shared a hearty laugh. Manfred turned to see what the cackling was about. He noticed the little girl from his transport trailing behind the group.

Her frazzled mother was busy calming the baby boy in her arms.

The girl had big blue eyes and curly, almost auburn hair. He quickly did the math. Could it really be that he hadn't seen his own baby in two whole years? What she must look like now, he thought. And the things she might be thinking. What gems would be coming out of her mouth? If only he could hear them.

He slowed down to keep pace with the girl's small steps, smiled at her repeatedly, and finally offered her his hand.

She timidly accepted.

The mother gave Manfred a relieved nod of appreciation.

Suddenly, Manfred remembered the photo in his coat pocket. He took it out and showed it to the girl as they walked. "See? *Meine Tochter,* my daughter," he pointed out. "She's small, with red hair, just like you. We've been separated because of the war, but I hope to see her again soon."

The girl gazed at the picture and watched intently as Manfred kissed it and placed it back into the breast pocket of his overcoat. She smiled.

Wiktor led us along the train tracks to the infamous selection ramp.

"Manfred would have walked this way...to the gas chamber," he said delicately. He pointed in a southern direction.

I was in denial. I needed to get the story straight.

"Wiktor, when we were at the ITS..."

*Otto handed me the last piece of paper.*

*"This is all I could find on Manfred," he said. "It documents his transport from Berlin to Auschwitz."*

*I felt gypped. I had come here for answers. "But, what happened to him once he got there?" I anxiously asked.*

*Otto hesitated. "I'm not sure how to tell you..."*

*I was growing impatient. "Tell me what?" I demanded.*

*"If he had been at Auschwitz long enough to receive a tattoo or put on a labor detail...that... Well," he stumbled, "that would have been documented."*

*"I don't understand." I felt my chest tighten. This wasn't what I wanted to hear. "What are you saying?"*

*Mike and Josh closed ranks to give me their unyielding support. Otto glanced at Frau Weisz. Her head dropped and she walked away.*

*"From our experience," he paused, "when the paper trail ends..."*

Wiktor looked at me sadly. "That would be my experience too."

My heart sank. Mike and Josh put their arms around me. I wiped a tear away.

"I think you should go on by yourselves. Take your time. I'll meet you back at the main watchtower when you're finished." Wiktor sprinted in the opposite direction.

We faced the gas chambers.

"It's a long walk," Josh observed.

I twitched my head back and squeezed my eyes tightly. I felt my body tremble. I tried to take in a breath. The air never made it to my lungs; it got uncomfortably stuck somewhere in the middle of my throat.

"Not long enough," I hissed.

Memel shadowed us as we approached Gas Chamber/Crematorium #2. The structure was mostly collapsed and surrounded by rubble.

"What happened?" Mike asked.

"The Nazis blew it up with dynamite before they left," I explained. "They didn't want anyone to know what they did here. It was a failed attempt to hide the evidence."

Josh spotted something unusual in the debris of the ovens.

"Was that...a *bathtub?*" he asked incredulously.

Mike and I thrust our heads in Josh's direction. Seeing what remained of a tub was confusing. I imagined that it must have been temporarily dumped there until the museum could put it in its proper place. Its presence made no sense. No sense at all.

Memel caught up. "Yes," he explained. "A bathtub. The kommandant used to like to take warm baths. The heat of the ovens warmed his bath water."

Mike, Josh, and I turned to see the expression on Memel's face. He couldn't possibly be serious, could he? Images of some faceless Nazi Kommandant humming Wagner to himself and soaping up his scaly back in a warm bubble bath while human beings—men, women, and children—were being annihilated in ovens just a stone's throw away would haunt me forever, I thought.

Memel must have realized that his tutelage lacked a certain sensitivity. "I'll be over there if you need me."

He slinked away.

Nervous but determined, I moved carefully onto the first step of the concrete staircase to the subterranean gas chamber. The chimney remains were still visible amongst the ruins. They stuck up out of the rubble like wobbly headstones. Behind me barbed-wire fence and a watchtower. Just beyond that, tall beautiful trees, the forest. I looked up—the sky was gray—then down, into the unholy abyss. Wiktor's voice played like a record in my head. "By the time the Nazis built Auschwitz-Birkenau, they had perfected extermination...no longer did the Zyklon B pellets fall from the ceiling and land on shoulders and the floor as at older, more experimental camps like Majdanek on the outskirts of Lublin. Here, at the world's most efficient killing center, once dropped from the roof, the poison slid down a strategically engineered pillar inside of which a large screw turned, more evenly dispersing the gas, killing Jews faster...hundreds dead in three to ten minutes. Nazis waited 20 minutes to be sure. They watched from round, hermetically sealed windows."

"Perfected...efficient...strategic...engineered...faster..."

I grew cold. Cries of the tortured souls radiated off the crumbled pieces of gas chamber and whooshed through my ears, piercing my aching brain.

There was only one thing I wanted to say, standing there, gripping that top step. And I wanted to shout it loudly. *Someone give me a bullhorn. Everyone must hear me, everyone should know. Wiktor! Memel! That*

*tourist over there contemplating the enormity of it all!*
*Fucking Adolph Hitler! Listen up, people!*

"I-AM-A-JEW!"

Where was He? I wondered. Where was God?

I felt a warm gust of air roll down off the trees behind me. It singed my skirt, seared my trembling bare legs, and pushed me forward and off balance a bit before it got sucked down into the vile vortex that lay before me. I went numb.

# Chapter 53

Manfred's group approached the concrete steps to go down into the disguised gas chamber. He noticed the chimney of the crematorium fiercely spewing its unholy consumption into the cold January air. He could hear a Nazi guard shouting orders from inside the brick walled corridor below.

"Take soap and towel!" the angry voice bellowed. "Hang your clothes on the hook and remember your number for later. *Kinder,* children, tie your shoes together so you can easily find them after your shower..."

The line continued to inch forward. The young blond mother and her baby headed down the stairs. Manfred felt a tiny grip tighten around his fingers. He looked down at the little girl. He had almost forgotten she was there.

"I don't know how to tie." She muttered the words apologetically.

He noticed her pretty red shoes. "I will help you."

They shuffled their feet until finally, the last of their group, Manfred and the girl stood perched at the top of the stairs.

In front of them loomed a tall chimney with ash shooting out the top. Behind them were, armed guards, watchtowers, and electrified barbed-wire fence, and just beyond that, beautiful snow-capped trees.

Freedom was just on the other side of the wire. It seemed so peaceful, over there.

Manfred released his hand from the little girl's grasp just long enough to retrieve his wedding band from under his tongue. Stealthily, he placed the ring back on his finger.

The girl watched intently. They teetered for one last moment at the top of the stairs.

He retook her hand, and they began their descent together.

"I forgot to ask your name," he said.

"Lyla," she whispered.

"Do you know *Shema*, Lyla?" he asked.

"*Ja*," she replied.

Manfred and the little girl prayed softly in unison as they disappeared down the concrete stairs.

"*Shema Yisrael Hashem Elokeynu, Hashem Echad.* Hear, O Israel, the Lord our God, the Lord is one."

Their voices trailed off until they could be heard no more.

*Frau Weisz returned with a large black rectangular, leather-bound book. On the cover, boldly imprinted in gold-leaf capital letters, was the word* Gedenkbuch.

*"Let's have a look in here," she gingerly advised.*

*Josh looked at the dark, ugly book and winced. Mike shook his head.*

*"What is* Gedenkbuch*?" I asked, knowing full well I didn't really want to hear the answer.*

*Otto opened the alphabetically collated record and turned right to the sizable section of surnames beginning with the letter J.*

*"A memorial book," he replied gently.*

*Otto flipped rapidly through a few pages, then stopped and sighed. He placed the book down in front of me. There it was, in black and white, three lines from the bottom:*

JOEL, MANFRED, FROM BERLIN, BORN 29.12.10, DECLARED DEAD, AUSCHWITZ.

Wiktor returned to guide us through a converted barrack housing various grim exhibits. By this time, he practically had to drag us. On our way, we passed the infamous Block 10, where inhumane medical experiments had been conducted on mostly women and children, especially twins; the prison within the prison where Nazis put Jews in carefully designed "starving" cells and tiny, dark, heated "standing" cells that no less than five beaten, famished prisoners had to crawl into and endure all night long; and the shooting wall between Block 10 and the prison, where someone could be shot for allegedly stealing a piece of bread or simply for target practice.

Inside the barracks, we found hundreds of personal documents and photos, then, behind glass, a wall of shorn human hair. We turned a corner to find another wall, of suitcases labeled meticulously by people who had been conscientious enough to try to not lose their precious possessions; a large hole resembling a drained in-ground Olympic-size swimming pool spilling over with dishes and bowls; rooms full of personal effects: hairbrushes, toothbrushes, eyeglasses, shaving supplies, cooking utensils, and Judaic ritual objects.  Finally, we arrived at a mountain of shoes...men's, women's, children's.

The walls felt like they were closing in.  It was nearly impossible to breathe.  Mike and Josh started to glaze over.  Might a belonging of Manfred's be amongst the spoils?

Something in the pile caught my eye.  A child's pair of red shoes, carefully laced together.

"How long did it take?" I blurted.

Wiktor was confused.  "Excuse me?"

"Manfred," I said, inexplicably fixated on the red shoes.  "According to your records, how long was he here?"

Wiktor stalled.

But I was desperate.  I insisted.  "How long?  Please, tell me, Wiktor," I begged.  "How much time did he have?"

He looked to Memel for permission.

"Tell her, my friend.  This is why she is here."

Wiktor could barely look me in the eye.

"Less than an hour."

The hand-cranked lift screeched as it slowly carried 48 dead bodies to the ground level to be thrown onto carts and wheeled into the massive ovens by the *Sonderkommando.*

The *Sonderkommando* were the unfortunate Jews chosen by the Nazis to do this most unthinkable task. The turnover rate of *Sonderkommandos* was unusually high because the Nazis used and then killed them to keep them from telling others what they were forced to do.

A very emaciated, worn-looking *Sonderkommando* wiped the sweat from his brow before it reached his swollen eyes. It was unbearably hot work by the ovens—work that went on all day, and all night. The ovens would be in operation as long as there were bodies, and there would be bodies as long as there were Jews. He lifted the lifeless form of the little girl onto the cart. As he moved her, he noticed a hand sticking out from the pile of carcasses.

On the hand was a familiar-looking ring.

The supervising Nazi slowly approached. "Check the bodies for jewelry and gold fillings," he shouted. "Push on bloated bellies. If you suspect a body contains swallowed diamonds, take it to the autopsy table."

The Nazi cracked a small whip and moved on.

The *Sonderkommando* shimmied the ring off the hand of the man. He examined it more closely, and soon enough, he recognized it. He had seen it taking a pounding from a bag at the gym and dripping with water from many a leaky pipe. His sunken, hollow eyes filled with tears as he dug Manfred's body out of the pile and cradled him. "Manfred..." the *Sonderkommando* cried, "come back! It's *me*, Erich."

Manfred and Erich had lost track of each other when they were each forced into hiding. By the time Erich's parents had been able to send for him, it was too late. Hitler had closed and locked the gates of hell on European Jewry, using the key to pry open cans of Zyklon B. Even Erich's parents' new American leader, President Roosevelt, sent about a thousand Jewish refugees onboard the ill-fated *St. Louis* back to their inescapable deaths on Satan's shores. There was no possible way to get him out.

Now, Erich was barely recognizable. Rail thin, a mere impression of his former self, he had aged beyond his years. Gone was the beautiful sable mane that had once been the envy of the masses. Those magnificent trademark locks had been unevenly shaved off his sorry head.

Clinging to his mentor's lifeless body, Erich wept.

Removing Erich's tearful grip, another, somewhat older, *Sonderkommando* with long droopy eyes carefully placed Manfred on the cart. He patted Erich on the head.

Erich fell to his knees as he watched the man roll the cart carrying Manfred's body toward the raging furnace. He was overcome with grief.

"Good-bye, my dear friend," he said quietly while secretly tucking Manfred's wedding band safely between the fabric of the Jewish star on his prison uniform and the uniform itself.

"Good-bye."

After leaving Birkenau, my husband, son, Memel, and I followed Wiktor through the main gates of the original, somewhat smaller, separate camp known as Auschwitz I. Reluctantly, we walked under the infamous sign, *Arbeit Macht Frei,* Work Makes You Free. At this point, we were completely spent, both physically and emotionally.

A small group of noisy tourists charged by. Wiktor was quick to admonish them. In Polish, he sternly scolded, "Quiet! You must show respect here." That was a side of him we had not yet seen, although at this point, it should have come as no surprise.

The embarrassed group immediately settled down and skulked their way into the camp. As I looked around near the camp's entrance, I noticed another visitor, a young man with long greasy hair, scarfing down half of a sandwich. *How could he?* I thought. I hadn't been able to eat for at least 24 hours in anticipation of this visit. And I was now certain that I'd never eat again.

Pointing over the shoulder of a young woman sitting on a curb and engrossed in a novel of some sort, Wiktor said, "This is where the Jewish orchestra was forced to play to calm new arrivals as they entered the camp."

Should I tap that disinterested gal on the shoulder and tell her? I considered it. But she seemed more engrossed in her book than in the horror that surrounded her, so I held my bitter tongue.

Making our way through the maze of Auschwitz, we spotted a large rectangular concrete hole. "What was that?" I queried.

With more experience than his age would seem to allow and, unlike Memel, with the utmost sensitivity, Wiktor sighed, "A swimming pool, for the Nazi guards. It got quite hot here during the summer months."

We were repulsed and speechless. Our response did not surprise him.

"Show them the festive yellow-and-black flyer," Memel said, salting the open wound.

"Festive?" I was sorry I had taken the bait the minute the word came out of my mouth.

"Inviting the guards to an SS dance," Memel cavalierly explained.

Wiktor shot Memel a dirty look.

"At Auschwitz?" Josh asked.

"Sure—" Memel started.

Wiktor cut him off, ending the conversation with, "I'm afraid so."

Wiktor led us to one of the camp's oldest prison barracks. Better constructed than the wooden horse stables of Birkenau, these barracks were made of concrete blocks and had been used by the Polish army years before the German invasion, but even these structures had only mud under foot and flat wooden, straw-covered plank beds, which, at their peak, had crammed in 500 to 800 people. I spied a plaque on the wall at the entrance.

"THE ONE WHO DOES NOT REMEMBER HISTORY
IS BOUND TO LIVE THROUGH IT AGAIN."
George Santayana

Inside, Wiktor directed our attention to a relatively small glass urn resting on a pedestal in the middle of a silent room. The steel frame was engraved, "1940–1945."

"In an effort to hide what they did, the Nazis spread most of the ashes of their victims around the land and in two nearby rivers," he lectured. "This is what was recovered from the ovens when the camp was liberated." He pointed to the urn.

I was floored. "One and a half million people were murdered here, and this was all they could find?" I shrieked.

Wiktor nodded. He put his arms around me and offered a warm, enduring hug. I looked into his understanding hazel eyes. Whereas Memel was often glib, naïve, static, removed, Wiktor with his quiet demeanor was patient, compassionate, and trustworthy. "Do you know the meaning of my name?" he asked.

I shook my head.

"Soldier of consolation. I hope I have done my job."

"You have," I said. "*Dziekuje.* Thank you."

Bawling, I reached into my backpack and pulled out some fresh yellow and white daisies I had purchased from a vendor on the street corner outside our hotel earlier that morning. Painfully, I laid the flowers at the base of the urn. Rummaging through my bag once more, I retrieved a few of our Kelly-green yarmulkes and a sheet of paper.

"Mom," Josh said, treading gingerly, "do you think he's in there?"

I wiped my tears and handed him a yarmulke. "Just in case," I said faithfully.

The men put on their skullcaps. I read from the paper and led them in a weepy version of the Mourner's Kaddish.

"*Yisgadal, Veyiskadash...*"

None of us looked back as we limped outside the gates of hell like wounded soldiers returning from the battlefield. Stumbling back toward the van, I tore through my overstuffed backpack, frantically searching for my cell phone.

"Rhonda, what are you doing?" Mike asked.

"I have to call Mom."

"You're not going to tell her—"

"Not yet. I just need to hear her voice."

"Now?"

"*Right* now."

# Chapter 54

*I*t was the first night of Passover in the small and crowded ghetto dwelling. Sarah was determined to give her girls a *Seder* despite their deplorable conditions and the clandestine nature of their activity. Her supplies were very limited.

The girls were seated around a shabby wooden table, at the center of which was a makeshift Seder plate.

"Sorry, girls, no matzo," Sarah apologized, "but I've been keeping *this* in a secret place."

She produced the traditional book for Passover, the *Hagaddah.* It was considerably worn, and the pages were the color of tea, but the familiar gold-and-red cover pleasantly surprised and even comforted the girls. Some of them gasped.

"Let's begin." She read from the book, "This is the bread of affliction..."

Sosia whispered to Pesia, "How does she do it?"

"She's good at hiding things," Pesia replied.

Frida turned to Devorah. "Where did she get the symbolic bone for the Seder plate? We haven't had meat since the Germans..."

Devorah cut her off. "From Mordechai," she said impatiently. "Where does she get everything?"

Frida was still confused.

"But where did Mordechai get it?"

Rivkah, 20, book-smart and mousy with pigtails, suddenly got alarmed. "Has anyone seen Effie?" she asked urgently, hoping she hadn't just solved the mystery.

Amongst the girls, there was a moment of horrible disbelief.

Frida and Devorah had a simultaneous epiphany. "Effie?!" they quietly cried.

Just then, Effie jumped up on the table. The girls breathed a collective sigh of relief.

Unfortunately, the girls' chatter climbed above a whisper and nearly disrupted the Seder. The culprits were embarrassed. Sarah chose to ignore their indiscretion. She turned the page of the *Hagaddah*.

"Chaya, you are the youngest, and therefore, it is your duty to ask the four questions."

Chaya looked hesitant.

Sarah encouraged her, "Please."

Soon, Chaya's lovely voice filled the room. She sang, *"Ma nishtanah ha layla hazeh..."*

Rivkah translated, "Why is this night different from all other nights?"

Under her breath, Devorah sarcastically retorted, "Do we even have to ask?"

Sarah finished the blessing over some black-market juice.

"...*boray p'ree hagafen.*"

Each one of them lifted their cup and drank.

# *Chapter 55*

*F*or many a night, the only light illuminating the old toolshed came from the iridescent moon and the twinkling stars in the otherwise black sky. That was about to change.

Only a few hours after turning in one evening, Regina and Tania, now age three, were as startled out of their sleep by the sounds of sirens as they were confused by screams coming from the main farmhouse.

Regina was pretty sure she recognized the predominant whirring as that of an *air-raid* siren.

Instinctively, Tania reached for her mother with one hand and clutched her doll tightly with the other.

The farm frau stormed into the diminutive shed and found Regina and her daughter clinging to each other on the single mattress between the draining spade and the grass sickle. The frau's face was pale, and her wiry white hair seemed to be standing on end.

"Follow me, quickly!" she ordered in a high-pitched squeal that neither Regina nor Tania had ever heard from her before. "The Allies are bombing Berlin!"

Regina grabbed Tania and followed the farm frau rapidly out of the rickety shed, racing past the rabbit cages and across a field into an underground shelter about 100 kilometers from the main farmhouse.

The frau's beefy husband was already there with a flashlight and a small radio. Not a word was spoken as the small group huddled closely together and listened to the sounds of bombs exploding all around them. The shelter rattled with each impact.

It wasn't long before an eerie silence replaced the sound of explosions. The farm frau and her husband were the first to venture out of the shelter to assess the damage.

About to resurface next, Regina turned to her daughter. "Stay inside until I tell you it's safe to come out," she instructed firmly.

Tania was concerned, but not for herself. "But *Mutti,* the rabbits..."

A few moments later, no longer able to heed her mother's orders, Tania peeked out of the shelter entrance like a gopher popping up out of its hole.

She saw her mother, the farm frau, and the frau's husband standing amidst the smoldering devastation of what was once a thriving family farm.

The air was thick with smoke, soot, and tufts of charred fur.

Little Tania cried out, "Where are all the rabbits?"

# Chapter 56

$S$arah, carrying a blanket-covered woven basket, had to step over the dead and dying who now littered the streets of Zgoda Square next to the Krakow railway station.

Small children with hungry, glazed eyes greeted her with silence and despair.

Nazi guards in their spit-shined boots guarded the train platform with their fierce guard dogs seated obediently by their sides.

Jewish policemen appointed by the Nazis, looking somewhat better fed than the rest of the Jewish population, patrolled the streets.

Sarah kept her distance and made her way farther down the tracks, where she tried to inconspicuously approach the platform.

Soon, she noticed others beginning to linger around the platform as well. Some carried sacks; others held baskets similar to hers.

The wool blanket covering Sarah's basket moved. She reached under and stroked gently.

"Hang in there, Effie," Sarah whispered. She could feel his little heart beating quickly.

"Mordechai instructed me to bring you for a reason. I'm just not sure yet what it is."

Effie relaxed at her touch.

Finally, a whistle sounded and the train pulled into the station.

The train doors opened, and people began to disembark.

As if on cue, cats were released from basket after basket all down the platform. Effie bravely joined the battalion of other felines, instinctively jumping from his basket and running past the Nazis' dogs.

"Effie!" Sarah shrieked.

The Nazi guards lost control of their dogs. The canines barked loudly as they chased the cats.

The Nazis ran after their animals. Chaos ensued.

People getting off the train swiftly unloaded sacks of food. Sarah suddenly realized what task she was meant to perform. She and the others filled their baskets, their pockets, and their arms with as much bounty as they could possibly hold.

She watched the others scramble back inside the ghetto.

Stealing a moment, she turned back for her constant companion, Effie. He was no longer in sight.

"Go with God, my precious little partisan," she said sadly.

Then, swift and noble, as Houdini's elephant had on stages across Europe in the earlier part of the century, Sarah disappeared, with her loot.

# Chapter 57

*I*t was dark. Regina and Tania ran between the towering, bare needle trees. Exhausted, they stumbled into a ditch. Every once in a while, in the distance, they could hear another bomb hit somewhere in Berlin and overhead, the opaque blackness would flicker with light for just a couple of seconds.

"Okay, *meine Tochter*," Regina finally said, "this looks like a good spot to make a camp."

"Camp?" Tania asked inquisitively.

"*Ja*," her mother answered. "We've never done that before, huh? Well, camping is what you do when you find a safe place to stay for the night in the woods." She looked around. "So, this ditch seems to be it."

"We'll go in the morning?" the child asked, needing reassurance.

"*Morgen Stunde hat Gold in Munde*," Regina said, recalling a German adage her mother used to repeat to her. "The morning hour has gold in its mouth, my darling. At daybreak, we will make our way back into the city to find another place to hide."

"But *Mutti,* it is cold here."

"I will keep you warm."

Tania tucked her doll under her body and curled under her mother in the ditch. Regina hovered over her like a mother bird sheltering the hatchling in her nest.

"I am so tired, *Mutti.*"

"Shhh, little bird. Go to sleep. *Mutti* will watch over you."

Tania settled in and closed her eyes.

Regina felt a drop, then another on her weary face. She used her own body as an umbrella to cover her slumbering daughter in the ditch. The cold rain droplets beaded up on her back and rolled down in all directions. Regina gazed hopelessly skyward, grateful to catch whatever landed on her quivering, parched tongue.

# Chapter 58

*P*ale yellow paint was curling up on the walls in the deteriorating parlor where Sarah was conducting a study group with several of the girls.

Food and water had become scarce in the ghetto, and the young women were beginning to look gaunt.

"Who do you think God was testing?" Sarah threw the question out to no one in particular.

"Abraham!" shouted Pesia.

"No, Isaac!" retorted Frida.

"Definitely Isaac," Devorah chimed in.

"Please discuss it," Sarah instructed.

As the girls engaged in a heated debate, Sarah moved to the kitchen, where a gaggle of other girls were peeling turnips and boiling a big pot of water in an attempt to prepare a meager meal.

"How's the soup coming?" Sarah asked, peering over the rim into the hot metal container. She managed to maintain a level of cheerfulness despite her disappointment in her own ability to provide more for the girls.

"Hand me a turnip."

Suddenly, Chaya and Rivkah sprinted breathlessly into the kitchen.  They were practically finishing each other's sentences.

"Mother Sarah," Chaya called out excitedly.

Rivkah handed her an envelope and explained, "This was just delivered for you."

"They said it's a prescription for Under the Eagle," added Chaya.

Sarah dropped the turnip.  "Did you say Under the Eagle?"

Clenching the envelope tightly, she bolted out of the house and into the crowded ghetto street.

Sarah's wide eyes darted up and down nearby congested alleys looking for a familiar face.  Chaya and Rivkah were right behind her.  They pointed.

"There!"

About ten meters down the cobblestones, Minka and Justyna were walking away, arm in arm.  The women turned back and briefly acknowledged Sarah, their flowing ankle-length skirts fluttering in the steady breeze.  Sarah returned a discerning smile.

Leaning against the wall, she anxiously tore into the envelope.

Inside was a note with instructions:

> *Tonight, 8:00 by the Vistula in the shadow of Beth Jacob.*

It was signed simply, *M.*

After dinner, the girls cleaned up and Sarah readied herself to leave. She discarded her armband and raced out the door.

Utilizing a maze of tunnels and underground passageways, she sneaked out of the ghetto and made her way to the river.

Hiding behind a large tree, she could see her beloved Beth Jacob School. Once full of light, laughter, and learning, it was now a dark, barren shell.

A noise startled her.

"Sarah, it's me."

The sound of his voice always calmed her.

"Oh, Mordechai, thank God. I was frightened half to death."

Briefly, they embraced. She relished the feeling of his warm arms around her and wished it could have lasted longer.

"Sit with me," he requested.

"But Mordechai, it's not safe. What if someone comes?"

"I'm willing to take that chance. Please," he begged. "Just for a moment."

She agreed, and they sat under the large tree by the meandering river.

"Promise me, Sarah, it's your last choice."

"I promise, Mordechai. If God shows us another way, we will gladly take it."

She composed her thoughts.

"The elders in the ghetto," she told him, "they need to protect their families. They want to live."

"Yes, of course."

"But the young adults only think about dying a most honorable death."

"Why do you think I joined the resistance?" he explained. "When I go, I plan on taking some Nazis with me." Mordechai exhaled, "I am ready."

She looked deeply into his eyes. "Then so am I."

Mordechai took Sarah's hand in his. "Sarah, I wish—"

She interrupted him. "I know, my darling. I sometimes think of what could have been. But I must take care of the girls, and you must continue to fight for all of us, for our people Israel. If we had more time, I would tell you how I have been searching for you all my life. A man such as you, a man of strength and conviction. A resolute yet tender man, a just and kind man."

"If we had more time, Sarah, I would *show* you how much I love you."

Sarah's face lit up. "Now I know why I never married," she said. "God was saving me for you."

She ran her willowy fingers around the contours of his chiseled chin.

"I love you too, Mordechai. May God bless you and keep you safe."

Mordechai removed the clip from the back of Sarah's hair, allowing her soft, loose brown curls to cascade down around her shoulders. He smiled. He had never seen her like that. She looked so beautiful.

He gently placed his hands on the small of her back and drew her toward him. His chocolate brown eyes seemed to melt in the moonlight. She touched his thick, wavy brown hair. It felt good and smelled better.

She palpated the warmth of his body against hers. His lips were firm and moist. Her eyes closed as she pressed her mouth upon them.

Finally, *finally* they shared a sweet, passionate, loving kiss.

Sarah felt as if she were floating above herself. He cradled her tenderly.

"If it is God's will that we don't survive," he said, "I will search for you in His kingdom. My soul will find your soul. We shall be together then."

"As it is meant to be," she avowed. "A heavenly union would be the reward for one that never had a chance in this world. I am a better person for having met you, my love."

She brushed her soft cheek against his. "Good-bye, my dear, sweet Mordechai," she whispered.

"Until we meet again, my beautiful Sarah," he replied.

They held each other tightly and stole one final, loving moment together under the glimmering stars.

Then he handed her a small, sealed bag.

# Chapter 59

*N*ight was enveloping the building that had once housed the Beth Jacob School for Girls.

Josh and Memel walked briskly back to the van. I lagged somewhat behind. Intuitively, Mike hovered near me.

"*Why* did we come back here this evening?" Memel asked Josh. Josh recalled how earlier in the day he had quipped that we were "pacing Europe" because of my repeated requests of our patient guides to revisit certain locations. Even Josh knew that Memel needed only a brief explanation.

"Mom wanted to see it one last time."

Memel and Josh each had one foot in the van when I called to them frantically.

"I need a minute!"

I walked over to the large tree and crumpled under it. Mike followed dutifully behind me. I put my head in my hands and began to weep.

My husband sat down next to me, lovingly put his true and muscular arms around my tired shoulders, and tenderly kissed me on the forehead. My rock was back.

The Vistula River meandered by.

# Chapter 60

With precise execution, Nazis stormed into the ruins of a bombed-out apartment building in central Berlin.

Their fierce dogs led them to a spot on the floor of one of the dilapidated flats on the ground level.

At the kommandant's command, the troops lifted the floorboards to reveal a handful of hidden Jews.

The Jews squinted and were temporarily blinded as daylight streamed into their subterranean hiding place.

Regina's sister Rosa was among them.

At gunpoint, each Jew was promptly ordered out and onto a waiting German truck.

# Chapter 61

PRAGUE, CZECH REPUBLIC

$S$till haunted by images of Auschwitz-Birkenau and suffering from various debilitating combinations of nightmares, insomnia, and migraines, we were more than ready to move on. Not sleeping or eating was beginning to take its toll. So far, the food in Europe was nothing to write home about. Fortunately for us, appetites had become a thing of the past.

Mike, Josh, and I welcomed the change when we landed in the next historic city on our itinerary and found ourselves following a well-educated, well-versed *female* guide. Our first *Jewish* guide as well since our journey had begun, petite, energetic, Julinka, spry and ripe at 61, would soon be running circles around us and eventually leave her weary traveling companions in a cloud of Czech dust. When Julinka wasn't guiding American tourists around her hometown of Prague, this little firecracker with a PhD in biochemistry chaired the law institute that had trained Iraqi judges for the Saddam Hussein trial. She was no slacker.

First up on her fast-paced agenda was a stroll through the neo-Gothic Maisel Synagogue.

From the outside, the synagogue looked like a whimsical white sand castle. The inside was just as fantastic.

On both the upper and lower levels, we were surrounded by beautiful Jewish artifacts: books, silver ritual objects, prints, and textiles.

"These are all of the things the Nazis stole from the Jews of Bohemia and Moravia," Julinka explained as we walked. "Each piece was carefully catalogued and methodically stored for the museum."

"Museum?" Mike asked.

"A museum of an extinct race," she clarified.

Josh was understandably confused. "What extinct race?" he questioned.

"Us," I answered flatly.

In a smaller, strictly off-limits room, I noticed a bookcase full of neatly hung velvet Torah dressings with handwritten German tags dangling from them.

A display of ornate silver Torah crowns had me in a trance.

"It's ironic," I added.

"What is?" Mike wanted to know.

"In a way, they kinda got their wish."

Josh chimed in. "What do you mean?"

"All of these old, beautiful synagogues showcase lots of *Jewish things*, but look around," I instructed. "What's missing?"

Julinka knew exactly what I was getting at. I detected a lamenting pain in her voice as she reluctantly provided the all-too-obvious answer.

"Jews."

Like a pixie, Julinka hurried us past throngs of tourists through the crowded streets of Prague's historic Jewish Town. We tried to follow her long, flowy apricot eyelet skirt and comfortable walking shoes but could barely keep up. Thankfully, she kept one pale, lanky arm in the air and flittered a few fingers from time to time so that we could ultimately locate her.

Mike felt for his wallet.

"Let me guess," I said dryly.

"Memel told him the pickpockets in the Czech Republic are the worst in all of Europe," Josh explained.

Julinka stopped in front of a tall, narrow relic of a building. The doors of the building were guarded by two armed Czech policemen.

"I think you're safe now," I whispered with a good-natured elbow to Mike's ribs.

He shrugged.

"This is the Jewish Town Hall," Julinka stated proudly. "Where we keep the records."

The lightbulb in my head flicked on. "Might they have information on Jews that were relocated from Germany?" I asked hopefully.

She smiled. "Yes."

I just about bounced off the structure's old stone walls. "Let's go in," I practically begged. "I have some research to do."

Julinka rained on my parade. "No one gets in," she informed us. "No one gains access."

I shot her a look. Mike and Josh laughed.

Yeah, I had heard that one before.

Minutes later, Julinka peeked her head outside the town hall's main entrance and motioned us past the guards.

"Okay," she said with some exasperation as she frantically waved us in, "I promised we'd be quick."

The rigid guards stood down. I tried to contain my satisfied grin as Mike, Josh, and I cruised past the sentinels and through the over-protected double doors.

After climbing endless stairs, we reached the simple and outdated office. There was a desk, a typewriter, and a card catalogue system from the late 1970s.

Two elderly women, one in her early sixties and one in her mid-eighties, kept the records. I smiled gratefully at the women. Neither of them smiled back.

The younger one brayed at Julinka in erratic Czech.

Julinka picked up a piece of scrap paper and a pencil from the desk and turned toward me. "Write what you know," she ordered.

I scribbled down the basics.

ROSA TYMBERG, SISTER OF REGINA JOEL,
BORN: DEC. 10, 1902, BERLIN, GERMANY.

Julinka looked it over and passed the note to the elder of the two women, who shuffled slowly to the card catalogue marked T.

Opening the drawer, she revealed hundreds of crisp pink 4x6 index cards. Within moments, she pulled one out and handed it to Julinka.

"Bingo," I said in a more audible tone than I had intended.

Josh and Mike seemed relieved.

Julinka passed me the card. My hands began to shake as I nervously accepted it. I couldn't wait to read this document and unlock its secrets. Here was a piece of the puzzle Otto didn't have back in Bad Arolsen. We were about to know more than him. I felt mostly apprehensive, but also somewhat scared.

Mike and Josh each held their breath as I scanned the card. Julinka was on standby in case I needed help translating. I didn't. My throat seized up, and my voice got caught in my dry mouth, but I managed to just barely squeak out the very last thing written on the card. It was the first Czech word I'd spoken since I entered the republic.

"*Terezin,*" I read out loud. My heart sank.

Julinka gasped. "It's Czech for—"

"I know," I said cutting her off sadly. "I know."

# Chapter 62

 he cattle cars unloaded outside of Prague.

Rosa and hundreds of other Jews disembarked in a state of confusion and were herded by Nazis into the main square of an old Czech fortress.

A crude wooden sign was nailed to the historic ancient wall that had originally been built to protect the city. It read in German: "*Theresienstadt.*"

ONE WEEK LATER

Rosa and a group of other fairly new arrivals were brought to a "dressed up" street that had been specially prepared for a visit by the International Red Cross.

The prisoners, like extras on a movie set, were instructed to stand in certain spots along the street.

An SS officer barked out orders as if he were the director of the film. "You and you stand here," he shouted as he broke up a group of Jews. "The three of you, together over there."

Deliveries of freshly baked bread and pastries were being brought into the "bakery."

Belgian chocolates were stocked on the shelves of the "sweet shoppe."

The street was colorful and lively.

The SS officer positioned Rosa in front of the mock bakery. "Don't move from this spot!" he ordered.

She inhaled. The smell of freshly baked bread had eluded her for quite some time, and she was hungry.

The officer addressed the prisoners. *"Achtung!"* He cracked a small riding crop.

"The visitors may ask you how you are doing, if you like it here, if you are being well cared for. All of your answers will be positive and brief."

His eyes were blazing. *"Verstehen sie?* Understand me?"

Rosa waited patiently. She listened as an assembled band of Jewish musicians tuned up in the main square. The SS officer had encouraged them to play jazz numbers despite the Nazis' vile distaste for the degenerate music of Jewish greats like Benny Goodman and Artie Shaw. Just this once.

Soon, a small group of Red Cross delegates, escorted by SS men, walked past Rosa and the others.

The area was serene and peaceful as the delegates passed facades of false restaurants and fake store fronts. The café looked pretty convincing, Rosa thought.

Well-dressed, healthy-looking Jews standing at their strategically placed spots pleasantly greeted the distinguished visitors.

Jewish mothers were pre-arranged, hand in hand, with their children. A group of young Jewish men, as rehearsed, kicked a soccer ball back and forth in the phony park.

Recently planted flowers were in bloom, and the area looked well maintained and spacious.

The Nazis smiled a lot and *kibitzed* with their guests.

Every once in a while, the delegates stopped to speak with an inmate. Under the watchful eye of the Nazis, the prisoners exchanged pleasantries and assured the visitors that their needs were being well met.

Finally, the delegates, satisfied with what they'd seen, shook hands with their Nazi escorts and departed.

"Everything here seems to be in order," a sharp-looking suited man with a Danish accent, who must have been the head Red Cross delegate, commented. "Thank you for your time, Kommandant."

Quite pleased with himself, the kommandant prodded, "*Gut, gut*...about your scheduled visit to Auschwitz..."

"Not necessary," assured the delegate. "We have all the information we need. Seems the prisoners are being adequately taken care of by the Nazi Party."

"I quite agree," added the smug kommandant.

As the delegates walked away, the kommandant whispered to his deputy. "As soon as we are out of sight, clear the street. Make sure every crumb is removed from the ghetto. Then get word to Auschwitz. Tell them they're not coming. Proceed with the exter- mination of the model family camp." His eyes lit up. *"Schnell!"*

After a few days, inside the thick fortress walls, the ghetto returned to a mass of neglected, starving, sick, and dying men, women, and children crying out in an unsanitary sea of overcrowded humanity. For Rosa and the others, the sweet smell of the make-believe bakery quickly faded into nothing more than a distant memory.

FOUR MONTHS LATER

Early one morning, a much thinner Rosa stood in formation at the Theresienstadt Appelplatz for roll call. She could hear the whistles of the trains waiting just outside the fortress walls. Her time was up.

Julinka led us through a narrow, dark cavern that stretched for about a mile under the fortress. There was plenty of ventilation. The air flowed easily from one end to the other. The walls were cool to the touch. Finally, we approached an offshoot catacomb that was filled with multiple wooden shelves; each shelf sup- ported six white paper boxes.

We were confused.

"What is this?" Mike asked.

"It's a re-creation," Julinka stated.

Josh and I moved in for a closer look.

"The Theresienstadt rabbis took great care to keep the cremated remains of the dead in paper boxes like these," Julinka explained. "Each was carefully labeled with the intent of giving the ashes back to the family for a proper burial after the war."

"But the camp was liquidated—" I contested.

Josh finished my thought. "What happened to the real ones?

"C'mon," Julinka motioned. "I'll show you."

As the sun set over the Eger River, Nazis unloaded thousands of white paper boxes from trucks and tossed them into the fast-moving waters.

Rosa's train passed by the river.

From a small window, she could see the Eger become a sea of white boxes, which gracefully bobbed up and down, gradually collapsing into the water, and, like a mass of tiny marshmallows atop steaming hot cocoa, melted away, one by one.

Watching, next to Rosa, through the same window were two men. One was an old acquaintance from Berlin, and the other was a well-known rabbi from Lublin, Poland, just outside of Warsaw.

"How many?" asked the Berliner.

"Twenty-two thousand," answered the rabbi.

A tear rolled down Rosa's sunken cheek.

"Look at the current," she noted. "This river flows back to Germany. They're finally going home."

Rosa wasn't. A sign on the outside of her train car read: "TO AUSCHWITZ."

Mike, Josh, Julinka, and I walked on a dirt path alongside the Eger River. Julinka was telling us a story.

"Some Jews asked their Czech neighbors to safeguard their valuables during the Holocaust. Many Czechs were resentful when those few Jews who managed to survive came back for their things after the war. It was not a welcome homecoming."

Plunderers. Accomplices. Sharp, hurtful words were stabbing me in the heart.

After a short while, we came upon a monument.

Julinka solemnly announced, "This is the spot."

Suddenly, the sound of people laughing climbed the riverbank and reached Julinka's discerning ear. She parted the trees to find the origin of the noise. Curiously, we followed her glance.

Down below, we spotted a handsome young Czech couple playing in the water with their two chocolate lab puppies. The man waded in the current. His jeans were rolled up to his knees, and what was left of a lit cigarette dangled from his goatee-framed mouth. The woman had long, wavy blond hair and sat alongside the river, with her feet in the water, enjoying a small picnic lunch. The puppies cavorted around her.

Julinka became enraged. She berated the couple. In Czech, she yelled, "Do you know what this place is?"

Surprised and unhappily interrupted, the couple glared at us.

"Yes," the skinny man with long brown curly hair challenged in his native tongue. "We know *exactly* what this place is."

He took the cigarette out of his mouth and purpose-fully extinguished it in the water.

His bobble-headed girlfriend giggled.

I freaked out.

"Son of a bitch!" I exclaimed. "I'm going down there!"

Mike and Josh tried to restrain me, but I was beyond the point of no return.

"Julinka, what can I call him that would really be an insult?" I asked in a crazy huff. "How about a stupid Slovak?"

Julinka tried not to laugh. "That would do it."

As I began to shout, my husband and my son covered my mouth and physically escorted me out of the park. Julinka followed close behind.

The ignorant couple shrugged us off and continued to frolic irreverently in the sacred waters.

# Chapter 63

JANUARY 5, 1945

$\mathcal{T}$he streets of Berlin were still.

The daily barrage of Allied bombings had become a welcome part of Regina and Tania's lives. With every explosion, they knew that Hitler was closer to defeat. But nothing could prepare them for the devastation they now encountered. Their beautiful city was in ruins. The roads were strewn with uprooted trees, collapsed gutted buildings, and wrecked cars. The sidewalks were clogged with bricks and pocked with craters.

Mother and now six-year-old daughter scrambled carefully over the rubble.

Silently, they sneaked behind buildings, down alleys and narrow passageways, carving a discreet path to the nearest S-Bahn station.

They stepped over bodies of dead German citizens who hadn't made it to safety in time—men, women, and children, their hair white from the dust of fallen plaster, their faces shrunken from hunger and fatigue, common folk who paid the price because Hitler was determined to fight to the bitter end, no matter the cost. The dried blood in their eyes had already turned to chalk.

Regina hurtled her daughter along.

As they turned the corner to approach the train station, they almost gagged on the stench. Here, the road was littered with dead and dying horses that had been carrying a truckload of ammunitions. There was no longer access to gasoline, so horse-drawn vehicles were now regularly moving military supplies around the city.

A woman was crouching over one of the horses in a praying position. As Regina and Tania got closer to the woman, they realized that she was slicing up the dead animal for food.

Tania gasped.

Regina scooped up her child and darted underground.

She knew there was no time to waste. Regina and her daughter swiftly navigated the S-Bahn station.

They came to a divided corridor. Regina struggled without her glasses to read the signs. Not sure whether to go right or left, she made a fast decision. Left.

Soon, she realized they were going in the wrong direction. Quickly, they doubled back.

Regina could hear voices and footsteps in the distance behind them.

Glancing over her shoulder, she saw two Gestapo officers.

She took her daughter's hand and yanked her forward.

Tania dropped her doll. "*Mutti, meine Puppe,*" she cried. "Mommy, my doll."

Regina didn't hear. She frantically pushed forward.

They arrived at the platform and nervously waited for the approaching train.

A middle-aged man in a gray silk suit walking ahead of the Gestapo noticed the doll on the platform and placed his briefcase down in front it. He waited for the Gestapo to pass and saluted.

"*Heil* Hitler!" he belted out.

The Gestapo officers responded in unison. "*Heil* Hitler!"

When the officers passed, the man used the back of his heel to kick the doll onto the tracks.

The officers exited in another direction.

Regina tightened her grip on Tania's hand.

The train whistled and pulled into the station.

As the Gestapo men exited the subway, another lone SS officer entered and noticed the mother and daughter waiting for the train.

The train came to a complete stop, and the doors opened. Regina and Tania stepped on. They chose the first two seats nearest the doors.

Regina reached into her coat pocket, pulled out a lipstick, and applied a fresh dark-red matte layer to her dry lips. She smoothed down her artificially colored platinum-blond hair.

Peering over her shoulder, she noticed that the train car was virtually empty.

The conductor made the announcement. *"Alles an Bord!* All on board!"

The doors closed and the train began to move.

Regina looked back at the platform. Through the window, she could see the man with the briefcase. He tipped his hat at her.

The train picked up speed.

Tania looked to her mother for reassurance. Regina gave her a calming wink.

Under the watchful eyes of her daughter, Regina reached into her purse and produced a navy-blue scarf. As she wrapped it around her head and tied it under her chin, she began to feel some of the tension leave her body. Her shoulders relaxed. She positioned her child on her lap and wrapped her coat around the girl so that from the back, it appeared as if a single Fraulein was sitting in that seat, not a mother and child.

Footsteps approached from behind.

Hesitantly, Regina looked up to see the lone SS officer from the station.

He smiled at her like an animal closing in on its prey, relishing the hunt.

She broke into a panicky sweat and looked into the confused, terrified eyes of her daughter. The young mother could hide it no longer. Her strength dissipated. Her face filled with fear, sadness, and despair.

Suddenly, the train ground to a halt. The lone SS officer motioned for Regina and Tania to go ahead of him. "After you, *Fraulein.*"

Regina and Tania had no choice but to stand before the train doors and wait for them to open.

Finally, the doors parted.

German shepherds barked loudly.

Regina and Tania nearly jumped out of their skins.

In front of the open train doors on the platform stood a gaggle of Gestapo policemen and several gnarling dogs.

This was it, the end of the line. The years of running, hiding, and subsisting through the kindness of others were over and Regina knew it. Finally, she heard the words she'd both dreaded and successfully avoided for so long. "Regina Joel," said the officer on the train, "you are under arrest."

# Chapter 64

$S$arah tried to stay upbeat as she led an after-din-ner discussion with the girls. The package from Mordechai weighed heavily on her mind, but not on her body, where she kept it discreetly hidden at all times. Despite their blighted situation, as always, the girls actively and enthusiastically participated in the dialogue.

"*B'tzelem Elohim*," quoted Sarah. "It means 'in God's image.' The Torah tells us that man is made in God's image."

"And woman?" asked Rivkah.

Sarah chuckled. "Yes, Rivkah. And woman."

"*Every* man and *every* woman?" Devorah wanted to clarify.

"Yes, Devorah." Sarah explained, "*Everyone* is cre-ated in God's image."

The girls were speechless. They all had the same question but everyone was simply too afraid to ask it. Everyone except Chaya.

"Even the Nazis?" she asked timorously.

The girls waited patiently while Sarah thought about her answer. "I suppose that even the Nazis *were* created in God's image—originally," she determined.

The girls looked surprised.

"Allow me to explain," Sarah continued. "When we say 'in God's image,' we don't mean physically."

Devorah added, "Obviously...none of us knows what the Almighty looks like."

"Right, Devorah," Sarah confirmed. "But we do know that God is a kind and loving God, and so it is in *that* image that we are all created."

Chaya was confused. "But not everyone is kind and loving."

"Certainly not the Nazis," declared Devorah.

Sarah explained further, "God has also given each of us free will. It is our *choice* whether or not to act in a kind and loving way, like God."

"The difference between us and the Nazis is that *we* have chosen to follow God's Holy Commandments," Devorah taught.

"And it is our responsibility to repair the world by bringing truth and justice to it," Sarah added.

Chaya got it. "Because God has given us an imperfect world?"

Sarah was relieved. "Yes, Chaya," she said. "God has most definitely given us an imperfect world."

Suddenly, ear-piercing sounds of shouting and screaming, then automatic gunfire came from the attached dwelling. The girls jumped to their feet in terror.

"My family!" Sosia shrieked. Sarah shushed her then motioned for the others to remain silent as well.

There was no place to hide, no time to run. They were trapped. The dwelling next door quieted quickly. Through the walls, Sarah and the girls could hear pieces of furniture being kicked and thrown around. Chaya began to choke on her fear. Devorah covered Chaya's mouth.

Sarah ushered the girls to a dark corner of the room. It wasn't long before the door creaked open. Slow, deliberate footsteps entered the room. In the moonlight, the girls could see shiny black boots.

The Nazi stopped mere paces from where the girls cowered. He shined a flashlight directly onto their frightened faces.

His evil voice enveloped every pocket of silence trapped in the unfortunate quarters.

"Good evening, *Frauleins*," Julian Schoerner said nonchalantly. "I've been looking for you."

The girls broke down in tears. Sarah positioned herself between the Nazi and her charges.

Schoerner roared, *"Die Juden sind hier!* The Jews are in here!"

A unit of Nazi officers, led by Bauer, stampeded noisily into the room. They immediately rounded up and arrested Sarah and the girls, shouting at them and forcing them out of the dwelling at gunpoint.

Schoerner victoriously lit a cigar as he watched the maidens get herded like cattle to a destination unknown.

# Chapter 65

*U*nfinished business and roundtrip airline tickets through Frankfurt led us back to Germany, where Rolf picked up speed on the Autobahn. I sat uneasily in the front passenger seat of the tidy German SUV. Mike and Josh were so exhausted in the back that they both started to nod off. I tried to write in my journal but soon felt overcome by an ever-amplifying wave of car sickness.

"Seems like we're going pretty fast," I said, trying not to sound like I was complaining. I looked at the speedometer. It read 160 km. "Josh, you got the calculator?"

Half asleep, Josh grunted.

"One hundred sixty kilometers," I pushed. "How many miles per hour is that?"

Josh did the calculation. "Ninety-nine point four two."

Needle trees and energy-collecting windmills lining the sides of the superhighway steamrolled by in a

Picasso-like blur. I settled my heavy skull on the rigid, mis-positioned headrest and, succumbing to the wooziness of it all, closed my bleary eyes.

Three hours later, Rolf was navigating us through a lovely Bavarian village. The homes were well kept and nicely manicured, with cheerful, colorful flower boxes in every window.

"We're almost there," he politely informed us.

I rolled down the window and glanced out in amazement. This beautiful, serene place, the peaceful little hamlet that time forgot, was the town nearest the notorious concentration camp known as Bergen-Belsen.

"They just went about their everyday lives," I uttered in disbelief. "Maintaining their homes, planting their gardens...how charming it must have been, living just down the road from hell." I sighed. "I will never understand."

I hated this place. I hated these people. I hated their flowers and their accents and their silent compliance. I was filled with hate. I shot Rolf a look of disdain.

"My father was too sick to fight in the *Wehrmacht*," he defended. "And I was only two."

Before long, we drove over some bumpy train tracks. I noticed a general store.

It seemed oddly frozen in time.

There were only six of them on the transport.

Regina, Tania, and two other frightened mothers with their sons, one about Tania's age and the other 15 years old, disembarked from the train in front of a general store. They scanned their surroundings in bewilderment.

German customers weaved in and out of the establishment.

Regina tried desperately to communicate with several of them.

"Excuse me..."

"Can you please tell me..."

"Where are we?"

*"Hallo..."*

No one would acknowledge her. Not one person would even allow eye contact.

A Nazi guard hit her with the butt of his rifle. *"Schnell!"* He ordered, "Onto the truck!"

Regina held Tania's hand tightly. She could feel her little girl shaking uncontrollably, but Regina couldn't make it stop. The group boarded the truck and went for a short, bumpy ride on a winding gravel road through a wooded area. As they approached the camp, Regina squinted to read the sign on the gate: BERGEN-BELSEN.

The group was ordered out of the truck and through the gates surrounded by high watchtowers and barbed wire. Regina looked around. They were somewhere in the forest. The air was cold and crisp. Regina shuddered. She had heard the rumors about Belsen. There were no gas chambers here, no labor details, no roads to build, no rocks to move, and only one oven to cremate the tens of thousands of bodies that had expired from starvation and disease.

At this place, she and her daughter would simply sit and wait for their turn to die.

Regina and Tania were directed into Block 22 in the women's camp. They entered an overcrowded horse stable filled with wooden bunks stacked like shelves.

The other women in the room resembled skeletons. They were either dead or dying and were packed in like sardines.

It was filthy, and the stench was revolting.

A few of the women noticed little Tania and shame-fully looked away. They were thinking, no doubt, of their own children who had been taken from them long before they arrived here. How had this one sur-vived? There was guilt, anger, and some hostility in the barrack.

Regina located an empty spot on one of the upper bunks and climbed up with Tania.

A baby on the next bunk cried out. Another rare, tiny survivor. A miracle, Regina thought—until his mother, lying contorted on straw, insane from starva-tion and dehydration, kicked him.

"Quiet!" she yelled in a cloud of confusion.

Horrified, Regina pulled her daughter closer. What was this hell they had entered? How long before she too would go insane?

"Why, *Mutti*?" Tania asked. "What did we do wrong?"

"We got caught, *mein kind*," Regina answered, resolved to remain strong for her daughter's sake. "We got caught."

The morning after their capture, Tania awakened first. She tried to rouse her mother with a gentle nudge. "*Mutti.* I have to go."

Regina only stirred. Tania crawled out from under her mother and climbed down to the mud floor. Unaccompanied, she left the barrack.

A few moments later, Regina woke up and felt around the berth for Tania. Realizing her daughter was gone, she panicked. "Tania!" she shrieked.

She climbed down from the top bunk and raced outside. Running down the path, passing several other barracks and a plethora of fellow prisoners, she called out frantically. "Tania! Tania! Where are you?"

Regina turned a corner and spotted the back of her daughter. Tania stood motionless in front of a small hill.

Regina was relieved as she approached her daughter from behind. "Oh, thank God," she breathed. Then she scolded, "Tania! You mustn't run away from me like that. I will take you to the latrines. Please never go alone again."

Regina moved closer to Tania, but Tania didn't answer. The little girl raised her arm and pointed at the hill. Regina looked at her daughter, then she looked more closely at the hill.

It wasn't a hill at all.

It was a mound of stiff, white, naked human bodies: men, women, and children, all of them lumped together, one on top of the other.

Regina recoiled in horror. She screamed and reflexively lifted her daughter, clinging to the child. She backed away from the mound of corpses and tripped over something, losing her balance.

She looked down and saw that she had tripped over a child's arm.

She tried to stabilize herself and tripped again. This time over a different child's leg.

She turned to see that she had been backing up to a shed that was so stuffed with dead bodies, the limbs of the victims piled inside could not be contained within and were preventing the doors from completely closing. A broken newborn cast atop the heap caught her unbelieving eye.

Dwarfed by the colossal clusters of carnage, Regina screamed again. Her futile cries struggled to scale the morbid landscape but remained coiled around her throat. A torrent of nausea overwhelmed her. "My God! This can't be happening! How could they do it?"

Regina ran back to the barrack with her daughter in her arms.

Tania was fixated on the piles of bodies over Regina's shoulder. She mimicked her mother. "How could they do it?" she repeated. Her precious little cadence now had a tone of innocence lost...eternally.

# Chapter 66

AUGUST 11, 1942

$C$haya, wearing a long, paper-thin white cotton nightgown, was exploring the many luxurious rooms of a spacious apartment in what had once been an upscale building outside the Krakow ghetto.

Inside one of the bedrooms, she found a beautiful antique writing desk. She opened the top drawer to reveal unembellished, ivory-colored stationary and an old-fashioned quill pen. There was an ink bottle in another drawer.

Seemingly at peace with herself, she settled in at the desk, carefully opened the bottle of ink, and began to compose a letter.

> My dear friend Mr. Schenkolewski in New York,
> Together with me are 92 girls from Beth Jacob. We were arrested and thrown into a dark room. We had only water. We learned David by

heart and took courage. We are girls between 14 and 22 years of age. The young ones are frightened. I am learning our Mother Sarah's Torah with them, that it is good to live for God but it is also good to die for Him.

The Nazis marched the maidens across the ghetto into an abandoned factory and ordered them into one cavernous room.

Sarah gathered them around her to study stories from the Book of David. She kept the youngest ones close by her side.

"God fulfills the wishes of those who fear Him," she recited. "God hears their cry and delivers them. God watches over all who love Him, but all the wicked, God will destroy."

The girls joined her in a chorus, "We will bless you, God, now and always. Hallelujah!"

Not long after, the girls fell asleep on the cold, hard concrete floor, using each other for support.

Yesterday, we were given warm water to wash, and we were told that German soldiers would visit us this evening.

A short time later, Sarah and the girls awakened to a clamor of Nazis hauling in tubs of water and soap.

As the Nazis departed, the last one to file out the door turned and commanded, "Bathe."

The girls complied with mixed emotions, happy to feel warm water against their skin and to feel clean again, but suspicious about the Nazis' motives for having them bathe. The girls sobbed softly as they were forced to undress and cleanse their trembling bodies.

Sarah bathed last.

When she was done, she sat up against the wall next to Chaya. Chaya laid her head to rest in Sarah's lap.

"Mother Sarah," Chaya asked, "when the time comes, how will we be able to do what we need to?"

Sarah had already solved that puzzle for herself. "Chayalah, my darling girl, remember when we studied Zechariah, Chapter 4, Verse 6? 'Not by might nor by power, but by my spirit, says the Lord.'"

Chaya nodded.

"Each of us may not be able to persevere alone," Sarah continued, "but together, we will be a force of nature. Survival comes in many forms."

Satisfied, Chaya closed her weary eyes.

The teacher stroked her student's baby-fine hair until they both fell asleep.

> Today, we were all taken to a large apartment with four well-lit rooms and beautiful beds. Everything was taken away from us, and we were given nightgowns.

In the middle of the night, Sarah and the girls were needled at gunpoint from their sleep and marched out of the ghetto and across the Powstancow Slaskich Bridge to the Aryan side.

They moved quickly and quietly.

Chaya caught up to Devorah, who carried her precious guitar. "Why do you think they are moving us in the middle of the night?" she whispered.

Devorah's fear kept her answer both brief and hushed. "Past curfew, no witnesses."

The girls were stopped in front of an upscale apartment building. They watched as Nazis exited the building with bags of silver Judaic ritual objects and other valuables and carried out original paintings by the masters. A Degas went by, then a Renoir.

A Nazi noticed Devorah's guitar. He grabbed that too. Devorah donned a brave face and resisted the urge to protest. She knew the consequence.

The loot, including the valuable instrument, was loaded into idling trucks, which soon departed.

Finally, the maidens were instructed to enter the building. The girls kissed a mezuzah on the doorpost as they entered.

A Nazi led the girls to four bright bedrooms with lovely beds dressed in expensive linens.

Draped across the beds were white cotton nightgowns.

"Put them on," he ordered.

The girls, including Sarah, tore off their armbands first, then did as they were told.


Chaya remained stoic as she folded the letter, gingerly placed it in an envelope, sealed and addressed it. She walked to the window and pushed the pane up with all of her might. Despite her greatest effort, the stubborn wood-encased glass would barely lift an inch. Chaya slid the envelope through the narrow opening and onto the outside ledge of the window. She closed the window and silently slipped out of the room.

A few minutes later, a gust of wind shot under the letter, gently lifting and floating it safely to the ground below, where it wedged between the white stucco wall of the building and a fairly large rock. Only the corner of the envelope was apparent, but even that was mostly camouflaged by its surroundings.

Meanwhile, in the well-equipped dining room of the apartment, Sarah and the girls found glassware and filled each glass about halfway with running water from the kitchen tap.

Privately, Sarah slumped into a richly upholstered burgundy velvet corner chair and seized a moment to speak with God.

"Are You here with us tonight, dear God? The monsters are coming to destroy Your children. We are not afraid," she affirmed. "We are not afraid..."

At the Cyganeria Club on Szpitalna Street in Krakow, Kommandant Julian Schoerner and his men were boozing it up. Their giddiness quickly rose above the smoke-filled room at the popular local pub.

Suddenly, Schoerner slammed his gun down on the table.

All eyes were on him.

"Whoever said war was hell never had the night we are about to experience!" Schoerner gleefully announced.

The men applauded loudly, hooting and hollering like a bunch of frat boys. Their smugness overwhelmed them.

"And so, in the name of *der Fuehrer,*" Schoerner continued, "the time has come to enjoy the spoils of war and claim our prize!"

He worked them up into a frenzy.

"*Herr Kommandant,*" his number-one henchman, Bauer, interrupted, "what about racial purity laws? Aren't we forbidden from having relations with Jews?"

Schoerner banged his fist on the table and salivated like a hungry wolf. "Don't worry yourself over silly race laws," he commanded. "This is war, and in times of war, all other theories are pointless." He concluded his rally by lifting his mug.

"*Heil* Hitler!" Schoerner heralded.

"*Heil* Hitler!" his men responded in unison, beer steins in the air.

The girls, dressed in their Nazi-issued white cotton nightgowns, were linked arm in arm around the elegant room. They each balanced a glass half-filled with water in their hands.

Chaya was sobbing.

Sarah's voice cracked. "I want you to know that each of you represents what is still right in the world. I love all of you as if I had given birth to you myself."

There was not a dry eye in the room.

Sarah and the girls recited the *Shema.*

"*Shema Yisrael, Hashem Elokenu, Hashem Echad.* Hear, O Israel, the Lord our God, the Lord is One."

Tears streamed down every cheek as the maidens hugged each other. Sarah took a private moment with each girl. She saved Chaya for last.

Dropping gracefully to one knee, Sarah spoke gently. "Are you ready?"

Chaya tried to be strong. She swirled her glass. "One more minute?" Chaya asked with great trepidation. Her voice was sweet like honey.

Sarah wiped the tears from Chaya's despairing yet lovely sky-blue eyes. She looked around the room, at her girls, at their beautiful faces. She beheld the purity and innocence of their souls. Her heart was heavy. "One more minute," she agreed.

Without warning, the peace was shattered when the door to the luxurious apartment was kicked open and the anxious Nazis stormed in.

The maidens trembled.

"So surprised, *Fraulein?*" Schoerner asked rhetorically. "You were expecting perhaps we wouldn't return?"

Schoerner and his men let out a collective, menacing howl.

Bauer, still drunk, was especially relishing this moment. "*Herr Kommandant,*" he giggled like a girl, "what have we here?" Clumsily, he lost his balance and bumped into the table, knocking over Chaya's glass. The maidens watched in horror as the drink spilled out and the glass was rendered completely empty.

"What the hell is going on?" Schoerner demanded.

Thinking quickly, Sarah lifted her glass. "A toast, *mein Kommandant,*" she proclaimed. "To the soldiers of the *Wehrmacht*, who would gladly defile these innocent maidens, adding to the spoils of the Reich and the immeasurable loss of the Jewish people."

The men weren't sure how to react to Sarah's blatant defiance. They waited for Schoerner's response.

Still rather tipsy himself, Schoerner considered the situation for an excruciatingly long moment. Then like a ravenous vulture, he swooped down on Sarah and forcefully pulled her toward him by her night-gown. The gown ripped, exposing her ample bosom. Schoerner practically drooled at the sight. Sarah swiftly recovered. He slapped her hard across the face. Sarah's drink almost spilled, but she saved it. The girls were terrified.

"We've had ours," Schoerner bragged. "I suppose it's only fair that you have yours." He chortled. "Make it fast, then," he added. "Spare my men from mounting shriveled-up *schnitzel*. Drink!" he commanded.

The other Nazis were amused. "Drink! Drink!" they repeated.

Chaya gazed at Sarah in despair. Her drink was well absorbed into the hand-woven silk tablecloth.

Without delay, Sarah passed her own drink to Chaya. Chaya silently protested, but Sarah insisted.

Outside, a white cat rubbed its head against the building's coarse stucco. He mewed and scraped at the ground-floor window.

The Nazis began pawing the girls. They were choosing their victims. Their evil laughter permeated every corner of the room. They unbuckled their belts and unbuttoned their trousers.

Sarah motioned to the girls to raise their glasses for the toast.

With a lump in her throat she declared, "We will drink to our suitors, and we will come to God Almighty and say, 'Here we are, pure and undefiled as befits the daughters of Jacob! Pray with us for our people Israel.'"

Bauer was beginning to sober up and spotted something odd on the table. He placed a monocle in his eye.

The expertly carved Bohemian glasses shook uncontrollably in the maidens' dainty hands.

Schoerner was losing patience. "Enough already," he demanded. "No more stalling."

*Sarah's father was teaching three of his daughters about Torah. Two younger sisters sat happily on Sarah's lap.*

She could see his face, she could hear his voice, she could feel their presence.

*"...as long as our choices sanctify God's name, they will be right. Remember it always..."*

Sarah found the courage to continue. *Her* voice was loud and clear. "The hour has come, and our souls grow quiet. One more prayer we utter: Brethren, wherever you are, say Kaddish for us, for the Jewish maidens."

Finally, Sarah gave the signal. The girls closed their eyes, threw back their heads, and drank.

# Chapter 67

ONE MONTH LATER

A shock of dyed strawberry-blond hair peeked out from a peasant girl's broad-rimmed straw hat. Under the hat, a well-disguised Hannah Weiss snooped around outside the large apartment building.

It was deserted. Gone were the Nazi patrols. All windows and doors were sealed shut. Through the windows, she could see that even the furniture was no longer there. The place had been stripped bare.

"I don't understand," she said faintly to herself. "According to all of the information on the street, they were brought here."

Hannah continued to peruse the grounds. Just when she was beginning to accept yet another dead end, she spotted the corner of Chaya's envelope sticking up from behind a sizable rock. She moved in to get a better look. Carefully, she lifted the letter, blew off the dirt, and examined it more closely. Her eyes began to well with tears as she realized what a treasure she had found.

Hannah tucked the envelope in her rucksack, threw the bag over one shoulder, and turned to leave. Directly in front of her sat a white cat with bright green eyes and a long tail.

"Effie? Is that you?" she asked.

The cat meowed a confirmation and rubbed against her leg. Hannah picked up Effie and glanced back at the apartment building one last time. Tears streamed down her freckled face. "We will tell the world what they did to us," she said. "We must bear witness."

From Hannah's shoulder, Effie played with a loose piece of straw on the broad rim of her hat. She nuzzled the cat and disappeared down the deserted alley with the letter protruding from her old, worn satchel.

# Chapter 68

*I*t was a raw, late-December afternoon on Szpitalna Street when Mordechai, Shimshon, Dolek, Eduard, Yitzchak, and several other resistance fighters rose undetected from the sewers and surrounded the noisy Cyganeria Club.

Peering through windows, they could see German officers inside celebrating Christmas. The officers were cackling, drinking to excess, and singing several off-key rounds of *Edelweiss*.

The Jews were armed with homemade grenades and revolvers.

Mordechai gave the signal. The resistance smashed glass and tossed the grenades through windows and doors, then quickly ran for cover.

Within seconds, the club exploded.

Tinsel, ornaments, and Nazi body parts were scattered about in the blast.

In the chaos that ensued, several rounds of shots were fired. There were casualties on both sides.

Shimshon and Yitzchak managed to escape. Dolek and Mordechai were hit.

Eduard checked on his comrades. "Dolek!" he cried out.

Dolek did not stir. He was dead.

"Rest in peace, brother."

Eduard ran to see about Mordechai. Although critically injured, Mordechai still had a spark of life left in him.

Eduard cradled his friend's bloody head. "Mo, stay with me," he pleaded. "Dolek is gone."

"Eduard, stick with the plan," Mordechai managed. "Bring supplies to Anielewicz in Warsaw. His partisans need you now."

"Please...don't give up," Eduard wept.

"I did what I set out to do. Carry on. Remember, God is on *our* side."

Those were Mordechai's last words.

Eduard heard the sound of rapid gunshots firing all around him.

Suddenly, Yitzchak and Shimshon popped up from under a sewer cover.

"Eduard, come on!" shouted Yitzchak. "Let him go."

"Save yourself," added Shimshon. "Mordechai and Dolek would want it that way."

Eduard took off his scarf and carefully placed it under Mordechai's head. He hugged his friend's still-warm body. He believed that, quite possibly, Mo could still hear him. "Good-bye, my friend," he whispered. "Don't worry. We won't give up the fight. We won't stop until we've defeated the Nazi beast. You will not be forgotten."

Eduard wiped the tears from his eyes and joined Yitzchak and Shimshon. Together, the three disappeared underground into the tunnels beneath Krakow.

Carnage littered the street.

# Chapter 69

*L*ike any other routine evening in New York City, winding down from his busy day, Meir Schenkolewski gracefully bobbed an herbal tea bag up and down in a sterling cup of steeping-hot water. When the tea was nearly crimson, he placed the used bag on a matching silver coaster beside his writing pad.

Positioning his wire-rimmed spectacles on the wrinkled bridge of his nose, he shuffled through the day's mail. An unconventional-looking letter caught his eye. He fingered the envelope, which was addressed to him in youthful handwriting. It was ivory and unembellished.

"Hmm..." he murmured to himself. "From Europe via Switzerland..."

He dropped two sugar cubes into the teacup and stirred. "The underground must have smuggled this one out," he thought aloud.

After examining the envelope thoroughly, he retrieved a slim silver letter opener with a mother-of-pearl handle from a neatly organized top drawer and carefully sliced the correspondence open.

Taking a sip of his hot tea, he began to read the letter.

We have a plan.

*As she wrote the letter, Chaya recalled how, moments before, downstairs in the dining room, Sarah had reached inside her nightgown and pulled out a small, sealed bag. Carefully, she had opened the bag, revealing its contents to the girls.*

In a few hours, all will be over. We are not afraid.

Yours,

Chaya Feldman from Krakow

Schenkolewski spilled the tea, burning his feeble right hand.

He fumbled for the phone on his desk.

# Chapter 70

*I*nside what remained of the infamous Bergen-Belsen concentration camp, Mike, Josh, and I stood before a giant mound of earth covered over by more than 60 years of organic growth.

A carved stone wall in front of the mound read in German, "Here Lie 5,000 Dead — April 1945."

To our right, another mound. "Here Lie 2,500 Dead."

To our left, more mounds, several extraordinarily large ones with walls engraved, "Here Lies an Unknown Number of Dead."

I placed some bright pink peonies by the stone marker. They offered a stark, perhaps too colorful, contrast to their grim surroundings.

"Bergen-Belsen is just one gigantic cemetery," Josh observed.

I remembered learning that the fear of spreading disease had caused the liberators to destroy the camp's infrastructure. I explained, "The British razed the camp after the war." They practically erased it.

We walked for a bit, passing a sign that described the prisoners' daily rations:

BREAKFAST
1/2 litre of herb tea
MAIN MEAL
3/4 litre of soup
SUPPER
bread or potato
20 dkg ersatz (imitation) coffee

"A forkful of veggie lasagna," Mike remembered.
"A forkful of veggie lasagna," I confirmed.
Josh dropped his head.
Mike was anxious to leave. "Let's get out of here."
The guilt consumed me. My son and my husband were suffering. They never wanted to come here, to this place, to any of these places. They had done it for me.
I looked into their overburdened eyes and agreed. We had seen enough.
"Where's Rolf?" I asked.
Josh pointed north. "I think I saw him go toward the chapel." We walked in that direction.
A few minutes later, as unobtrusively as possible, while Mike and Josh waited outside, I entered the chapel and spotted Rolf hunched over in an anchored chair nearest the eternal flame. He looked devastated. Respectfully, I knelt down next to him.
He pulled a damp hanky from his pocket and wiped his moist brow. "I didn't know that my people committed such atrocities against your people," he lamented.

"You didn't know?" I repeated in utter disbelief. The words nearly spun my head off my body.

I felt physically ill, as if the fever of typhus that eventually wiped out most of the prisoners of Bergen-Belsen, including Anne Frank and her sister, Margot, had come over me too. I suddenly felt all of the pain and suffering of so many crushing down on me, suffocating me. I felt trapped. A primal scream surged up inside of me like an angry geyser, but I corked it with every ounce of strength I could conjure, and then some.

I realized that my blame would not find a home with Rolf. After all, each of us only knows what we know and the rest has to be learned. Here, in the twilight of his life, Rolf was still learning. He gazed at me in earnest.

"I think I have learned more truth in my short time with you than in all my 66 years as a German," he said, his voice cracking.

That was all I needed to hear.

My anger subsided and was replaced with compassion for the folded, broken old man before me.

Managing a half smile, I rubbed his crumpled shoulders. I assured him, "Better late than never."

# Chapter 71

APRIL 15, 1945

*A* small convoy of troops charged through the German countryside. The land was serene and picturesque: rolling green hills, cows grazing in the meadows, birds chirping. It was a beautiful spring day in Deutschland.

On the lead jeep, a Union Jack attached to the antenna flapped in the gentle breeze.

Commanding officer Colonel Trevor Wright, a young, athletic, decorated British soldier was speaking into his walkie-talkie. His straight lemon-yellow hair flapped about under his beret. He consulted a map.

"Roger that," he said. "I can't believe the *Fatherland* still has such beautiful scenery," he added in a snarky tone. "Looks like the Allies missed a spot or two. Over."

A deep, strong voice came back over the walkie-talkie. "Blame it on the Russians. Over."

"Copy that!" Wright chuckled, his muscular body quivering as he laughed.

The joke was short-lived.

The men in the jeep began to notice a foul stench in the air.

Colonel Wright forgot to take his finger off the talk button.

"Dear God," they heard him say on the other end.

The convoy pulled up to the main entrance of Bergen-Belsen.

Behind the barbed-wire fence were drawn faces with big hollow eyes—women and children, mostly. Living skeletons.

Behind them, 10,000 unburied, naked corpses formed large latticed piles.

More bodies filled huts, sheds, and makeshift tents.

The British soldiers disembarked from their vehicles. Some of them fell to their knees and vomited.

"Round up the monsters who did this," Wright commanded.

Those soldiers who were able to hold it together began rounding up Nazi guards.

Colonel Trevor Wright stood, rifle drawn in his Royal army stance, scanning the scene. He seemed unable to move.

The voice on the walkie-talkie was desperately trying to communicate with him, but he failed to hear it. At this moment, he was deaf to everything: the cries of the prisoners, the retching of his men, the protests of the Nazi guards who remained.

In fact, as he looked around, everything seemed to be moving in a sort of muted slow motion. Until a tiny, dirty hand tugged on his punished fatigues.

Glancing down, he snapped back into reality.

It was Tania, her once adequate clothing now tattered. She was filthy and emaciated and hadn't had food or water for at least six days. She was covered in big fat white lice. Her weathered face made her appear much older than her nearly seven years. "Life" at the camp had surely aged her.

In a soft, sweet voice, she uttered, "*Meine Mutti.*"

Tania took Wright by the hand and led him through the camp. The little girl's legs and feet were black, sore, and blistered.

The soldier's well-worn boots picked up mud and debris as they moved past and over chalky white, bone-thin human limbs.

Wright stumbled as he tried to avoid stepping in human excrement.

They walked past the dead and the living dead suffering from typhus, tuberculosis, starvation, and dysentery until they reached a shabby wooden barrack.

The skeletal survivors there begged him for water.

A small voice called out, "*Kommen,* come."

He remained locked and loaded, just in case.

Stepping over two dead bodies to get in, the colonel noticed that they were a mother and child huddled together. They had expired in that position days ago, he figured. He choked on the horror, his disbelief, his sorrow.

Wright pulled a hanky from his pocket and covered his mouth and nose. The odor was unbearable. Cautiously, he followed the girl inside.

She walked him past dead and dying people lying on every shelf of the five-tiered bunks.

The hut was not as crowded as it had been when Regina and her daughter had first arrived, making more room for those who managed to cling to life.

In the rear of the barrack, the girl pointed to a woman lying listlessly on the top bunk. The woman was skin and bones, barely breathing, had a high fever, and was clearly hallucinating.

Although at death's doorstep, the woman perked up discernibly when she spotted Wright. "Darling!" she said excitedly. "Where have you been? It's been so long. The baby and I missed you...Manfred..."

Tania stroked her mother's lice-infested, bleached-out hair. She looked up at Colonel Wright with her sweet, sad little face. "*Meine Mutti,*" she introduced.

# Chapter 72

O n our way out, we traversed the blood-soaked earth of Bergen-Belsen one last time, then paused at the museum to sign the guest book. I wrote, "I'm here. I am a witness to the evil that nearly destroyed you. They did it, they know, we all know. The evidence is everlasting."

Mike added to the note: "Your strength gives us strength."

But there was still one thing left to do.

Rolf, Josh, Mike, and I took our seats in the small, dark, empty media room. An 8mm film tickered rapidly through an old projector. All-too-familiar images of what the liberators found when they arrived at the camp flashed on the screen in front of us: confused survivors, barely alive, unable to change the frozen grimaces on their shriveled faces; Nazi guards once so brazen and self-righteous cowering before their British captors; and a handful of grief-ridden women mustering up enough strength to chide their oppressors who were collecting the cadavers and throwing them into large open mass graves. It was too painful to watch.

And then, softly, between the sounds of the victims shrieking in different European dialects and the British soldiers bellowing at those who had operated this catastrophic Armageddon, I heard it. Glancing over my left shoulder to the very last seat in the row, my eyes confirmed what my ears were hearing. Sitting all by himself, wrapped in a twisted labyrinth of guilt and shame, Rolf was crying.

The movie flickered on.

The day after liberation, another new flag waved gently in the breeze over Bergen-Belsen. It was pure white with a large red cross dead center. International Red Cross personnel ran to and fro, escorting the barely able-bodied survivors to barracks that had been transformed into makeshift hospital wards.

A volunteer holding Tania's hand guided her to the far side of the camp.

On the way, they passed a British officer with an 8mm movie camera. He was filming interviews with Nazi guards. Each guard was required to identify himself or herself: rank, file, and serial number.

Just behind them, other Nazi guards and some local townsfolk were being forced by the liberators to do the grim work of carrying dead, naked, atrophied bodies to a giant pit and tossing them in. Standing over the pit were several survivors. The survivors cursed the

Nazis in German, Dutch, Polish, and other languages. They cried, yelled, derided the Nazis, and demanded justice.

The volunteer ushered Tania to a Red Cross truck and offered her some water. Instinctively, the girl tried to gulp as much as she could.

The volunteer stopped her. "*Slowly*, little one," she urged. "You're so dehydrated. You must only sip."

A British soldier approached with a few more of the youngest victims. "Not many little ones left," he noted.

The volunteer advised the soldier, "We're still losing them. Another 500 people each day. Either the typhus is too far gone, or we give them too much heavy, fatty food and their starved bodies just can't handle it. Their stomachs are bursting."

The soldier seemed aware. "The SS cut off their food and water supply and ran about a week before we got here," he explained. Then he instructed, "Control their intake. Start with liquids, then slowly build up to solid food. Let all the volunteers know."

Later that day, Regina, in a white hospital gown, lay in a single bed in a converted barrack attended by Red Cross nurses. She was just beginning to recover from typhus. Had the war lasted another day or two, she most certainly would have died.

For now, she was restless.

"*Meine Tochter, meine Tochter,*" she shouted. "Please, someone find my daughter!"

A pleasant-looking young nurse heard the commotion and rushed to Regina's bedside. She tried to calm the woman. "It's okay, Regina," she said in her most soothing voice. "We found her. Somehow, you two got separated and we thought she was an unaccompanied child. But with the help of the soldiers, we were able to bring you two back together." She motioned to the next bed.

"She's right there. See? She sleeps."

Regina looked over to find Tania curled up in the fetal position and sleeping peacefully.

"Thank God and thank you!" Regina breathed. "Please, may I ask a favor?"

"Of course."

"Move her closer."

The nurse obliged, pushing the beds together.

Regina succumbed to the sleep-inducing combination of fever and medication, but not before cradling her daughter's tiny, precious hand in her own.

A Red Cross nurse posted a list on a sizable cork board outside the hospital doors. "New list!" she announced loudly as she secured it with a metal pushpin.

Word spread quickly through the hospital corridors and the surrounding grounds.

From her bed, Regina awoke to hear other survivors clamoring. "Please God," a woman's voice prayed aloud, "let my Moishe be on the list!"

Regina glanced over at Tania, who was still fast asleep. She dragged herself out of bed and slowly made her way to the posting. Her distempered body could not keep pace with her anxiety. By the time she got there, a crowd had converged on the board.

One by one, the ragged, worn, recovering survivors fell away. Some wept in disappointment; others cried tears of relief and joy.

Regina, with hope against hope, apprehensively approached and carefully read over the list.

She recoiled.

Then, in her moment of intense disheartenment, she thought she recognized the welcome sound of a familiar voice.

"Regina? Is it you?"

Was she still hallucinating? Regina turned and was both stunned and elated to see her dear old friend. "Erich!" she cried out joyfully.

They embraced.

Frail and pale, Erich was dressed in Red Cross donations. The clothes hung heavily on his gaunt frame. There was not a trace left of his unbridled exuberance. He was no longer a boy, yet only a shell of a man. His sallow face managed a smile at the sight of her.

Regina looked him over, desperately searching his ravaged eyes for any bit of information. "Manfred?" she begged.

Erich motioned to Regina to sit with him on the steps of the hospital barrack. His barren eyes filled up. He found it impossible to speak. Instead, he took Manfred's wedding ring out of his pocket and placed it firmly in her palm. Erich held Regina as she collapsed into his arms.

She screamed an agonizing scream. *"Nein!"*

Her wails echoed throughout Bergen-Belsen. They joined the chorus of suffering that, even after liberation, still permeated the thick, dense air.

Red Cross trucks idled in line just outside the main gates of Belsen as they filled up with orphaned Jewish children.

Volunteer staff and non-staff alike helped the children load onto the trucks.

A woman with her arm around a scraggly little boy argued with a Red Cross official who was seated at a folding table near the trucks.

The indifferent official stared callously at his clipboard.

She pleaded with him. "But you have to take my child," she insisted. "I have relatives who can look after him. *Bitte!"*

He rolled his eyes. "I am sorry, madam," the official repeated. "I already told you, only *orphans* qualify for this trip." He brushed her off. "Please step aside."

The woman grabbed her child by the hand and stormed away in a flurry of frustration.

Regina and Tania were next in line.

Regina signed the papers and nervously handed them to the official. He looked them over, carefully. As she had learned to do for the entirety of her six and a half short years, Tania held her mother's hand and remained positively silent. She had perfected this skill, as her very life had always depended on it.

"Relationship to the child?" the official asked curtly.

Regina tried to remain as pleasant as possible. "Sister," she answered affably. "She's my little sister." Regina flashed him an ingratiating smile.

He stamped the papers.

Regina walked her daughter to the already full truck. There was enough time for a brief embrace, then she handed the child a small rucksack. After everything they had endured, their parting seemed almost inconceivable.

"You'll stay with cousins until I can find us a place to live and a country that will have us," Regina promised. "Don't worry, they will take good care of you. *Verstehen*, understand?"

Tania nodded an uncertain confirmation.

Regina got down on her knees and held her daughter tightly. "I love you, Tania. You are going to have clothes to wear, food to eat, and a warm, safe bed to sleep in at night. You will go to school, make friends, learn, laugh, and play. You'll finally have a chance to live a normal life, something you haven't experienced since..." She paused as she realized the gravity of what she was about to say. "Since the day you were born."

That was the sad truth. Fear was all this child had ever known.

Regina kissed her baby girl. "I'll send for you as soon as I can," she vowed.

A tear stained Tania's little cheek. She hugged her mother once more, then approached the truck nearest her. A dark and once dashing man hoisted her onboard next to the other frightened children.

The man locked the back of the truck and gave it two quick pats. "Ready!" he shouted.

Tania could see her mother blowing kisses.

The truck engine revved.

The man backed away from the dust kicked up by the departing trucks. He stood near Regina and the others who sadly waved good-bye to the children.

Regina broke down. The man noticed and put his arm around her. "There, there," he said, trying to comfort her. "She'll be okay. You are doing the right thing. This is no place for a child."

Regina wiped her tears and pulled herself together. "This is no place for a human," she said impatiently. "Do I know you?"

He sheepishly retracted his arm and politely extended his hand. "Forgive me," he said. "Allow me to introduce myself. My name is Eduard. Eduard Weksler. I am from Poland. I was a weaver before the war..."

The hum of the trucks getting farther away could be heard in the distance.

Regina let Eduard accompany her back toward the front gate of the camp.

"After the Nazis murdered my parents in front of me, I escaped underground and joined the resistance," he continued. "I fought in Poland with some of the bravest young Jewish men and women..."

At the front gate, a British Army crew was changing the Bergen-Belsen sign.

They covered the words "CONCENTRATION CAMP" with a wooden board that read, "DISPLACED PERSON'S CAMP" and hammered it into place.

Regina and Eduard passed through the gate, still engaged in ardent conversation.

"And by the way, I agree with you," Eduard stated. "This *is* no place for a human."

Regina managed a smile.

Regina and Eduard were sitting on a bench, exchanging sad personal histories and learning the harrowing details of how the other had ended up at Belsen when Erich suddenly bounded toward them, eager to impart some good news.

"Regina!" Erich almost sang, barely able to contain his excitement. "Your sister, Rosa! I think she's here! Her name was added to the list!"

Regina's dim eyes grew lighter. Her near disbelief was apparent. "Rosa?"

Regina, Eduard, and Erich bolted breathlessly through the camp to the infirmary and bounced past the doors. Regina stopped a doctor. "Rosa?" she queried enthusiastically. "Rosa Tymberg?"

The doctor pointed to a room full of recovering survivors.

Regina's anxious eyes scoured the beds. Finally, in the far corner of the room, she spotted her older sister and was naturally overjoyed to see her but shocked and saddened by the appearance of an evidently tortured face.

Rosa's right hand was wrapped in bandages, and her feet were under a heavy warming blanket. Her eyes were closed. Her head was shaved. Pointy bones were visible under her skin, and she had a number tattooed on her left forearm.

Unable to contain herself, Regina squealed with delight, "Rosa!"

Rosa forced open her weary eyes. "Regina?" she whispered. "It is really you?"

Eduard and Erich stayed back to allow the reunion.

Regina cried tears of sheer joy.

"Yes, sister. It's really me!"

"Regina...you survived!"

Rosa noticed Eduard and Erich. "Tania?" she asked hesitantly.

"She's fine," Regina assured her. "On her way to London as we speak."

Regina gently hugged her battered sister.

"Oh thank God, thank God!" Rosa repeated.

Regina became indignant. "God?" she scowled. "I'm not so sure about God anymore. Where has He been? I didn't see Him amongst the corpses here in Bergen-Belsen. I don't think Manfred saw Him in the gas chamber at Auschwitz..."

Rosa wept. "Oh, Regina, I am so sorry."

Regina pressed on. "On the list," she continued. "It says you were in Theresienstadt *and* Auschwitz. Was God there for *you*, Rosa?"

Even lying there in bed, in that condition, like the eternal flame glowing bright in the darkest corner of the room, Rosa clung to her optimism. "Smile, *Liebchen*," she said as she always had. "We are still here. *Am Yisrael Chai.* The Jewish people live."

Regina assisted her sister as Rosa tried to sit up.

Rosa searched Regina's beaten eyes for one more piece of information. She feared the answer, but she had to know. Ultimately, she mustered the courage and asked, "What about our oldest sister? Regina, tell me....what happened to *Sarah?*"

# Chapter 73

*I*n the middle of the night, the phone rang at the Joel flat.

"*Hallo,*" Regina answered anxiously.

The voice on the other end cracked. The reception, however, was atypically crystal clear.

"Frau Joel," she heard the voice say, "it's Meir Schenkolewski of the Beth Jacob Movement calling from New York."

Regina sucked in her breath.

"It's about Sarah," he continued.

Regina listened. Her hands shook as she finally hung up the receiver.

She looked woefully at Manfred.

"We have to go," she said.

She picked up a framed photo on the telephone table. It was a happy snapshot of the three sisters when they were young: Sarah, 20, with the two little ones, Rosa, 11, and Regina, 5, contentedly sharing their big sister's lap.

The healthy hue drained from Regina's courageous face. A tear traveled down the curve of her pallid cheek. Manfred pulled her close and held her tightly.

Around the dining room table, inside the large apartment, Schoerner and his men were still feeling the residual effects of the alcohol they had consumed just a short time earlier.

The Nazis wickedly built their chant into a resonating crescendo. "Drink! Drink!"

Sarah gave the signal. All at once, the girls threw back their liquid.

Bauer reached for the empty capsule on the table. As soon as he picked it up, he realized what he had found. The monocle fell from his eye and hit the hardwood floor. It shattered upon impact.

"*NEIN!*" he shouted, alerting his accomplices.

The beasts drew their weapons.

Much to the Nazis' surprise and disgust, one by one, the maidens began to die.

Sarah, her eyes floating in tears, had visions of the girls the way they were before the occupation: full of joy and life, dancing, singing, praying, carefree by the river, studying Torah, and performing a holiday show. Then she remembered them bravely defying the Nazis during the occupation, smuggling goods and feeding the hungry.

CLICK.

The sound startled Sarah back to the here and now. She was staring down the barrel of Schoerner's gun.

Quickly, she brought the room into focus, her heart breaking as she looked around. All of the girls were dead.

Her gaze found her precious Chaya lying still, collapsed over the end of the table. She wailed.

Schoerner raised his pistol and whipped Sarah until she bled.

He put his sweaty, angry face within inches of hers. He pressed his gun to her forehead, right between her devastated, glazed blue eyes.

He roared like a cheated monster. "Your turn to die, *Jude!*"

Sarah mustered up one last act of defiance. She closed her eyes and recited the Mourner's Kaddish.

*"Yisgadal, Veyiskadash, she'mei raba..."*

Outside the large apartment building, the sound rung out for miles. A single gunshot. It echoed.

Startled by the loud noise, Effie took off down the street like a cat out of hell.

# Chapter 74

*I* closed the file and noticed a round, white analog clock on the wall. Three hours had passed. Only three hours? I remembered the map in the lobby labeled 1933–1945. Indeed, it felt more like those 12 years had passed.

Through my uncontrollable tears, I focused outside the window at the beautiful greenery surrounding the International Tracing Service. It hit me. It was no accident that this place was hidden and so completely isolated. Because in that moment, I felt isolated too.

I looked at Otto. "Now you know," he said.

I cried. For Sarah and the girls, for the Joel family, for all those who had suffered and died at the hands of the Nazis because of their faith. And then, I cried for me. The truth hadn't only been permanently etched into my memory, it had been forever carved into my soul.

It took a moment for me to compose myself.

Mike was sniffling. Josh had his head in his hands.

"Copies?" I asked despondently.

"Absolutely. I will put it all on a CD and send it to you."

I reached into my backpack and handed Otto some euros. "For shipping...and your trouble," I insisted.

Otto refused with an iron-clad grip on my wrist. "Every survivor has a story," he said, making the most deliberate eye contact anyone has ever made with me. "These vaults are full of them. We are just the keepers, but this..." He held up the file.

"This story belongs to you."

# Chapter 75

uilt in the late '80s, my recently updated suburban kitchen was bright, spacious, and comfortable. With its warm butterscotch walls crowned in
eggshell dentil molding and deep coral and gum-leaf
green accents, it had a beautiful new laminate floor
that mimicked a classic shade of wide-paneled cherry
hardwood, a heavy walnut kitchen table with high-
backed cushioned chairs that perfectly matched the
cabinets, and the latest coffeemaker that brewed one
gourmet cup at a time. It wouldn't be long before I
would upgrade to modern stainless appliances and a
highly polished, more practical granite countertop in
complementary caramel tones. I had it all figured out.

I fixed a pitcher of unsweetened iced tea.

Bubbie sat motionless at the table. In front of her
was an open laptop. She stared nervously at a blank
screen.

Shayna joined her grandmother and offered her a
quick, obligatory hug and kiss. Even though Bubbie

knew the show of affection had become somewhat forced as Shayna had grown into those moody teenage years, it didn't stop her from always lighting up around her beautiful granddaughter. Besides, she was sure that Shayna would eventually grow out of it. Her mother had.

"How was camp, my Shayna Maidele?"

Shayna smiled one of her typical post-braces, perfectly straight, pearly white toothy grins.

"Great, Bubbie! I hooked up with a cute boy!"

Bubbie looked surprised.

"Made out," I translated for my mother. Which I promptly followed up with "TMI," admonishing my fresh and often inappropriate daughter.

As I was about to apologize to my mother for my teenager's lack of discretion, Bubbie looked at Shayna and asked, "Just one?"

"*Oy vey*, you two!" I shrieked as Bubbie and Shayna had a good laugh. It was good to see them bonding, even if it was at *my* expense.

I poured Bubbie a tall glass of tea and offered her a packet of her favorite artificial sweetener. Then I pulled up a seat next to my mother and daughter and followed their collective gaze into the darkened monitor.

I shimmied the mouse. Bubbie spotted something unusual on the screen. She moved in for a closer look.

"You have email from Bergen-Belsen?" she asked incredulously.

"Yeah," I answered flatly. "They need more information."

Bubbie and Shayna were astounded.

"From you!?" they asked in unison, their voices each raised about an octave.

I chuckled. "Apparently, I now know *more* than they do. I'm helping them update their records."

"Regarding what?" Bubbie wanted to know.

"Regarding *you*," I informed her.

I peeled an unlabeled CD out of its plastic holder and inserted it into the computer's disk drive.

"*Mutti*, how's your German?"

Bubbie sighed. "Good enough I suppose, *meine Tochter.*"

I looked into my mother's tired eyes. "Are you ready?"

Bubbie put on her bifocals. "Yes," she said. "I believe I am."

Shayna and I each put an arm around Bubbie's weary shoulders. I was always relieved to see Shayna do something sweet and selfless. It was a glimpse of the thoughtful young lady that she was becoming and I was thrilled to see *this* Shayna making more frequent appearances.

I pointed to the screen. "Click right there."

Bubbie slid her gold charm bracelet down her age-spotted wrist and glided her old, crippled hand over the mouse.

She clicked.

*I*t was a warm Sunday morning in May. The class-room was vivid and cheerful, decorated from wall to wall in student artwork celebrating Israel's upcoming Independence Day. As had become my yearly ritual at Temple B'nai Abraham Religious School in an affluent suburb of Philadelphia, I planted my 20 sixth-grade students in front of an outdated 36-inch television monitor. Today was Yom HaShoah, the annual Day of Remembrance of the Holocaust. This was the time of year I was required to delicately introduce the horrors of the Holocaust to my fresh-faced students who had spent the past eight months focusing on prayers, Jewish life-cycle events, holidays, traditions, and Jewish history since the Babylonian era.

This would be the heaviest lesson by far, which, the students would admit, would have the most impact and leave a lasting impression.

I peeled open a white cardboard video box and inserted a VHS tape into the antiquated machine. I always held my breath with these old things. Thankfully, the device didn't eat it.

We sat in rows and watched a testimonial produced by the Shoah Foundation.

On the TV, an unseen interviewer was asking an elderly woman in her late 80s with bleached blond hair, large eyeglasses, and a thick German accent to describe her captivity in Bergen-Belsen.

At the bottom of the screen appeared the name Regina Joel Weksler.

"It wasn't a hill at all," Regina described on the videotape. "It was bodies, dead bodies, piled one on top of the other..."

The students were riveted by her eyewitness account.

I dabbed the corners of my eyes. Although I had seen the footage a hundred times before and I had been in the room on the day it was taped, it still tormented me to hear her story. I remembered begging Regina relentlessly to record her story, if not for herself, for posterity— for her grandchildren and for their children after them. My persistence eventually paid off, and although Regina had passed away a few years before, I was still able to bring her into my classroom, introduce her to a new crop of eager students each year, and have her help me teach the unfortunate lessons of the Holocaust.

A couple of the girls sitting on either side of me offered a concerned, sympathetic look. I put an arm around each of them and returned a maternal smile. These were *my* kids. Much like Sarah, year after year, I formed a bond with these children as if they were my very own. Nothing was more important to me than, as our rabbi liked to call it, "making Jews."

The interviewer on the video asked, "When you first went into hiding, where did you go?"

"To a woman who used to clean our apartment," Regina responded. "And she took us in."

I used the remote to pause the video. I had some information I thought the students might find interesting. "You know," I interrupted, "I actually met the woman who risked her life *and* her children's lives to hide them from the Nazis. Would you like to hear that story?"

The students responded with enthusiasm. "Yeah!"

"All right," I said. "Gather round."

The kids moved their chairs to form a semicircle around me.

"When I was in college, I studied for a semester in London. My British cousin decided to take me to Germany to see his mother and meet someone very special..."

*BERLIN 1984*

*I was barely 20 at the time. Tall and hardened, 56-year-old Josef Tymberg brought me into a small, modest flat in a busy, clustered section of the city. I was looking very '80s with my big hair, parachute pants, and denim-and-red Michael Jackson "Thriller" vest. My collar was up.*

*On a crisp white sofa, two petite elderly ladies sat smiling and chatting away in German like two twittering little birds. Clearly, they were old friends.*

*One of the women, familiar to me and 82, wore a colorful satin patterned dress with coifed red hair and oversized glasses. She had a number on her left forearm and a permanently deformed right hand, an ever-present reminder of sadistic medical experiments she had endured at Auschwitz's notorious Block 10, of which she would never speak.*

*The other, older, woman had her gray hair pulled straight back into a tight bun and wore a simple blue and purple floral housedress. An olive-green blouse peeked out at her neckline. Her skin was flawless. There were no lines on her 90-year-old face. She was plain but remarkably beautiful.*

*Joe and I approached the women. They looked at me with wide eyes.*

*"Mother," Joe said, "it's Rhonda."*

*I practically mowed down the woman with the red hair.*

*"Tante Rosa!" I squealed, enormously happy to see my great-aunt.*

*"Oy! Rhondala," she said in her thick German accent as she maintained her balance. "I'm so glad Josef brought you here. I haven't seen you since you were a baby!" Rosa had no young people in her life anymore, and she gazed lovingly at me as if I were her only hope for the future.*

*"I have warm regards for you from my mother and grandmother," I told her. She beamed.*

*Joe led me to the other woman, who was smiling brightly.*

*"Rhonda," he began to introduce, "this is—"*

*As I shifted my attention to the elder woman, I suddenly felt swollen with awe and gratitude. I dropped to my knees. Before me sat the most righteous person I would ever meet. I couldn't believe my eyes. My heart pounded. This frail, unassuming old soul had the chutzpah to take on the Third Reich. At this moment, I knew what courage was, and I would surely never be the same.*

*"Frau Tietze," I uttered with sheer reverence. I took her aged hands gently in mine.*

*All of my feelings bubbled to the top. I had so much to say, and it all wanted to gush out at once. Somehow, none of it seemed sufficient.*

*"It is an honor to meet you. If it weren't for you, I wouldn't be..." I began to rattle on in English.*

*Frau Tietze looked confused.*

*"German,* Liebchen, *German!" Tante Rosa pleasantly instructed.*

*"She doesn't speak English," my cousin Joe explained. "Do you know any German?"*

*I thought about it for a moment. "I know one word, but it's the only word I really need," I told him.*

*I looked deeply into Frau Tietze's compassionate blue eyes. I was completely overcome with emotion. "Danke," I choked.*

*Frau Tietze smiled even bigger. A tear rolled down her sweet, humble face.*

My students were attentively listening to my story. One of my overachievers, Stella, 12, eagerly shot up her hand.

"What does *danke* mean?"

"It's German for 'thank you.'"

The children got silent. I saw the need to take a breather. "Okay, you guys," I blurted, "What do you say we take five upstairs, then head into the sanctuary and wait for the family Holocaust program to begin?"

"Okay."

"Cool."

I put my arms out. "Hugs!" I demanded with a wink.

Happily, the students came over and gave their teacher one serious group hug. I could see that a few of them still had heavy hearts. It was time to lighten the mood.

"Last one up is a moldy bagel!" I announced.

The students froze, unsure whether I was kidding or not. Taking the lead, I dramatically bolted out of the classroom. Feeling somewhat relieved, the kids followed me out in hot, giddy pursuit.

The sanctuary was full of students and their parents. I was seated in the front row with my family. Bubbie, Mike, Josh, and Shayna had decided to join us for this special program.

A couple of kids seated behind Josh and Shayna were talking. Josh turned around first. "Quiet!" he demanded.

"Respect!" Shayna added. Brother and sister fist bumped.

Mike gave me a wink. I beamed proudly.

A diminutive, spirited gentleman with a thick Polish accent, Sam Kaytes, 80, was at the mic, concluding his story of surviving Auschwitz.

A large free-standing menorah with Hebrew writing on it adorned the *bimah*. Bubbie leaned in to me and whispered.

"What does it say on the giant menorah?"

I whispered back, "Not by might nor by power, but by my spirit, says the Lord."

Mr. Kaytes continued, "And so when people ask me how I survived Auschwitz when more than a million other Jews did not, I tell them mostly...it was luck. And maybe, He," he said, pointing up, "had other plans for me."

That was my cue. I was the lead teacher on this particular program. When it came to Holocaust education, many of the other teachers in the religious school would often defer to me. They would ask to co-teach a program, tap some of my resources, or consult with me on the best way to broach the subject with the children without frightening them to death. I was flattered that they considered me to be somewhat of a Holocaust scholar, and humbly, I was only too happy to help them meet their educational needs.

I approached the mic, covered it with my hand, and whispered a request to Mr. Kaytes. He nodded.

"Sure," he said. "Absolutely."

I spoke into the mic. "Good morning. For those of you who don't know me, I'm *Morah*, teacher, Rhonda. In my classroom, the students learned that when a Jew was sent to Auschwitz, if he wasn't gassed right away..."

I looked cautiously at my mother. Bubbie seemed to be holding up, so I continued.

"That is to say, if a Jew was going to stick around for any length of time and be forced into slave labor, the first thing the Nazis did was remove his or her identity."

I felt a lump form in the back of my throat. This was really hard.

Shayna offered me a tissue from the official "rabbinical box of tissues" that the rabbi kept on the *bimah* for parents making speeches to their children on their Bar or Bat Mitzvah day.

I gladly accepted it.

Forcing myself to go on, I continued, "They would take your clothes, your hair, even your name and replace it with a number. That number was tattooed on your forearm."

I looked back at Mr. Kaytes for affirmation. He signaled me to continue. He was still on board.

"Mr. Kaytes has such a tattoo, and he has graciously agreed to show it to us now."

Mr. Kaytes began to roll up his shirtsleeve. The room was pin-drop silent. He broke the ice. "If I had known I'd be doing a striptease," he joked, "I'd have brought my music!"

He got the desired response. Everyone breathed a huge sigh of relief. There were even a few chuckles. This guy knew how to work a crowd.

Mr. Kaytes bared his forearm and revealed the horrid tattoo. Parents and students alike gasped.

As the audience gaped at Mr. Kaytes's unfortunate souvenir from his wretched past, he whispered to me. "Does you mother wish to speak?"

I looked at Bubbie, who was fidgeting with her gold charm bracelet.

"No," I said sadly. "She hasn't spoken about it in 70 years. I don't think she's gonna start now. Let's wrap it up."

Mr. Kaytes began to close his presentation. "Well," he concluded, "I thank you for having me here today. I believe there are refreshments in the back of the room..."

People started to get up from their seats.

Concentrating on her bracelet, Bubbie separated out the baby and anniversary charms that represented the special milestones in her lifetime and fingered a man's gold wedding band. It was an heirloom.

Then, unexpectedly, in a barely audible tone, Bubbie simply said, "I will."

Abruptly, Mr. Kaytes halted the end of the program. "Just a minute please," he said into the microphone, causing everyone to sit back down.

I looked at my mother incredulously. "Mom?"

To my amazement, Bubbie stood up and slowly approached the mic. My family was in shock. Whispers spread like a brush fire throughout the sanctuary.

I did the only thing left to do. "Parents and students, fellow staff members, I'd like to introduce to you another Holocaust survivor...my mother, *Tania*."

I sat in the empty seat between Josh and Shayna.

The room quieted. All eyes were on Bubbie Tania. She cleared her throat.

"Excuse me," she said. "I'm a bit dry."

Mr. Kaytes handed her his glass of water and then sat down on the other side of Mike.

She sipped. Slowly. Just as the Red Cross volunteer had coached her in Bergen-Belsen when she was a starved and dehydrated little girl tasting freedom for the first time, I thought.

"Thank you," she murmured.

Finally, she summoned the courage to speak.

"I was born in Berlin about a month before *Kristal-nacht*, the Night of Broken Glass..."

I felt the tears roll down my face. Tightly, I grasped the hands of each of my children, linking the next generation of my family together, and sighed, "Let the healing begin."

# Epilogue

*I*nsecure about learning a new language and start-ing a new life in a new land, Rosa Tymberg chose to stay in Germany.

Travel restrictions prohibited her from seeing her son again until his wedding day when he was 19, in London.

Josef Tymberg built a life in Manchester with his devoted British wife, Jose. They never had children and eventually retired to the Canary Islands.

Rosa found Frau Tietze after the war, and the two women remained close friends for the rest of their lives.

With quotas for Jews from other countries filling up quickly, Regina Joel was stuck in the Bergen-Belsen Displaced Persons camp for almost five more years.

During that time, she married Eduard Weksler and bore him a son, Robert.

Tania was nearly 11 years old when she was reunited with her new family. A few months later, they were granted asylum in America.

The mid-1950s brought a permanent return to platinum blonde for Regina. This time by choice, *not* necessity. Her new American friends affectionately nicknamed her "Marilyn." She got a kick out of that.

In 1961, surviving sisters Regina, Rosa, Hanni from England, and another sister, Erna, who had survived Nazi-occupied France, saw each other in America for the first time since the end of the war. The happy occasion was Tania's marriage to Herbert Fink. It took a wedding to finally reunite the sisters, and *The Philadelphia Inquirer* and *Reuters* covered the story.

Although Regina questioned her faith in God after the Holocaust, she continued to practice and celebrate her Judaism throughout the rest of her life.

Regina Joel Weksler lived to be 94.

Now in her 70s, Tania comfortably divides her retirement years between Philadelphia, Pennsylvania, and Delray Beach, Florida.

She has three children and seven grandchildren. One of them is named after her father, Manfred.

Following the heroic attack on the Krakow Cyganeria Club, 20 Jewish resistance fighters were killed in battle with the SS. They took some Nazis with them.

By 1945, the Nazi and subsequent Russian occupations had successfully shut down 167 European Beth Jacob schools for girls.

In the years following WWII, new Beth Jacob schools were opened throughout Europe and launched across Israel, South America, and the United States.

New generations of Beth Jacob girls continue to pray and study together to this day.

The veracity of the story of the Beth Jacob maidens has long been a subject of debate. The undisputed

truth is that while Hitler systematically murdered six
million Jews, countless others chose death over dis-
grace.

This story is dedicated to the memory of them all.

Spoiler Alert: Please don't look at the pictures until after you have finished reading the book.

Regina's family: children from left are baby Regina, Hanni, "Zenta" (nickname), Oskar, Rosa, Heinrich, and Erna with their parents Channah and Josef, Germany 1909.

Regina and Manfred's wedding day, Berlin 1936.

Rosa and Josef Tymberg, Berlin 1930.

Tania, age 2, and her puppe (doll).

Eduard made his way to Warsaw where he continued to fight in the Resistance. This is the Aryan ID card and the work permit which he resourcefully obtained identifying him as a Polish conductor named, Bronislaw Wojciechowski. Although all of his personal information had been falsified, it is actually Eduard in the photo. Over the next three years, even after the fall of his comrades during the Warsaw Ghetto Uprising, armed with this assumed identity and unbridled courage, he successfully smuggled Jews out of Warsaw. In doing so, Eduard saved countless lives.

The mermaid insignia symbolizes the city of Warsaw.
Eduard's documents courtesy of Robert Wexler.

ÚSTŘEDNÍ KARTOTÉKA — TRANSPORTY.

Oscby došlé do Terezina z různých území

*Tymiberg Rosa*

rodná data ........... 10. 12. 1902

adresa před deportaci ...........

Deportace na východ: Číslo ........... **Ep** *1470*

*TEREZIN* *OSWĚTIM*

dne ........... 8. X. 1944

(*původní transportní číslo:* *14.784 – I/113 – 16. 6. 44*

*BERLIN – TEREZIN*

III.

Rosa's pink card.

Ce Certificat est delivré par le HOME OFFICE, LONDON, et expire le_____
sauf prorogation de validité.

The present Certificate is issued for the sole purpose of providing the holder with identity papers in lieu of a national passport. It is without prejudice to and in no way affects the national status of the holder. If the holder obtains a national passport this Certificate ceases to be valid and must be surrendered to the issuing authority.

Le présent certificat est délivré à seule fin de fournir au titulaire une pièce d'identité pouvant tenir lieu de passeport national. Il ne préjuge pas la nationalité du titulaire et est sans effet sur celle-ci. Au cas où le titulaire obtiendrait un passeport national, ce certificat cessera d'être valable et devra être renvoyé à l'autorité qui l'a délivré.

Surname / Nom de Famille } _____ JOEL

Forenames / Prénoms } Tania.

Accompanied by / Accompagné de } child (children) / enfant (enfants)

Remarks / Observations }

The undersigned certifies that the photograph and signature hereon are those of the bearer of the present document.

Le soussigné certifie que la photographie et la signature apposées ci-contre sont bien celles du porteur du présent document.

Place and date of birth / Lieu et date de naissance } 29. 9. 1938 BERLIN

Occupation / Profession } SCHOOL GIRL

Present residence / Résidence actuelle } 73, ASHR.GT. LONDON

*Maiden name and forename(s) of wife / Nom (avant le mariage) et prénom(s) de l'épouse }

*Name and forename(s) of husband / Nom et prénom(s) du mari }

DESCRIPTION / SIGNALEMENT

Height / Taille } 4' 8"

Hair / Cheveux } FAIR

Colour of eyes / Couleur des yeux } BLUE

Nose / Nez } NORMAL

Shape of face / Forme du visage } OVAL

Complexion / Teint } PALE

Special peculiarities / Signes particuliers } NONE

CHILDREN / ENFANTS

Issued at / Délivré à / Date: LONDON

Signature and stamp of authority issuing the document. / Signature et cachet de l'autorité qui délivre le titre.

17 DEC 1948
HOME OFFICE

Fee paid / Taxe perçue : 5 : 0 / 7 : 6

Signature of Bearer—Signature du Titulaire.

British ID papers issued to Tania, age 10, while she remained in London.

THE SUNDAY BULLETIN, PHILADELPHIA, SUNDAY MORNING, APR.

# *Girl, 11, Teaches English to Mother And Stepfather in DP Family Here*

Edward Weksler, 33-year-old weaver from Poland, pores over his English lesson with his step-daughter, Tania (right), acting as teacher at their home, 626 McKean st. Mrs. Weksler, whose first husband, Tania's father, died in a Nazi concentration camp, holds son, Robert, eight months

**By PHILIP B. SCHAEFFER**

*Of The Bulletin Staff*

The after-supper scene around a table at 626 McKean st. looked familiar: a father and mother helping their school-age daughter with her lessons. But there was a big difference.

Tania Weksler, a freckle-faced, blue-eyed girl of 11, was patiently teaching English to her mother and stepfather, Regina and Edward Weksler. The whole family, including eight-month-old Bobby, are among the 1,000-odd displaced persons being cared for by the Philadelphia Committee for New Americans.

*Sponsored by AJA*

dish but only little bad English," added Weksler. "I try hard to learn fast."

The cheerful South Philadelphia apartment of the Wekslers is in striking contrast to their former home, the infamous Nazi concentration camp at Belsen, Germany.

On that April morning in 1945 when British Tommies broke through the barbed wire surrounding Belsen, Mrs. Weksler—then the widow Joel—and little Tania were among the 30,000 living skeletons in the camp.

**A Grim Reminder**

Some 10,000 bodies were strewn about the streets or piled high outside furnaces awaiting cremation. Yesterday Mrs. Weksler examined

had met Weksler. He had gone to the camp in the hope of finding some of the 30 missing members of his family.

An ex-Polish soldier, Weksler had been captured by the German army and sent back to a Polish ghetto. Then, while being transferred to an extermination camp, he managed to flee. He went to Warsaw, assumed the name of Branislaw Wojciechowski and became a trolley conductor. After hours, he was an officer in the anti-Nazi underground army.

**Were Married at Belsen**

In 1947, the Wekslers were married in Belsen, which had been converted into a DP center. They decided to try to gain admission to

Role reversal. Tania helps her parents with their lessons. The Philadelphia Bulletin, April 1950.

Four sisters separated by the Nazis chat with Tania Wexler (lower left) whose wedding next Saturday brought them together after 25 years. They are (from left) Tania's mother, Regina, of 4829 N. Marshall st.; Mrs. Erna Moschkowitz, Paris; Mrs. Luxenberg, Berlin; and Mrs. Hanni Erlich, London.

Sisters reunite for Tania's wedding.  Front page of The Philadelphia Inquirer,
March 5, 1961.

### Wedding Reunites Four Sisters

Mrs. Regina Wexler (second from left) and her three sisters are reunited at her home in Logan as the family gathers for the wedding of Tania Joel Wexler (left) and Herbert Fink next Saturday. Aunts of the bride-to-be are (from left) Mrs. Hanni Erlich, of London; Mrs. Erna Moschkowitz, of Paris, and Mrs. Rosa Luxenburg, of Berlin. Sisters, all of whom were in concentration camps during World War II, have not been together for 25 years.

The Philadelphia Inquirer, March 5, 1961.

# A Reunion For Sisters Who Faced Nazis

PHILADELPHIA (Pennsylvania), Monday.

MRS. HANNI ERLICH, 55, of Edgware, Middlesex, flew in here to attend the wedding of her niece and was reunited with three sisters she had not seen since Nazi terror separated them in Berlin 28 years ago.

Mrs. Regina Wexler, 48, now living in Philadelphia, decided that the wedding of her 22-year-old daughter, Tania next Saturday would provide the opportunity for the long awaited reunion.

Mrs. Erlich and 61-year-old Mrs. Erna Moschkowitz, from Paris, arrived at International Airport here on a Transatlantic flight. An hour later the other sister, 58-year-old Mrs. Rosa Luxemburg stepped off another aircraft from West Germany. Her home is in West Berlin.

The four sisters last saw each other in 1933 when they separated to escape Hitler's anti-Jewish pogrom.

With her husband, Mrs. Erlich fled to England. The other three were not so lucky and all spent some time in Nazi concentration camps—Reuter.

From a London newspaper, March 1961.

Tania's wedding with Regina, Tania, Eduard, and Robert. March 11, 1961.

Tania and Herb's wedding portrait, Philadelphia, March 11, 1961.

From left: Rosa, Frau Tietze and Rhonda, Berlin 1984.

Josef and Jose Tymberg, London 1984.

Regina celebrating her last Birthday. October, 13, 2002.

Tania 2012.